An Irresistible Temptation

An Irresistible Temptation

A Cavallo Brother Romance

Elsa Winckler

TULE
PUBLISHING

Chapter One

ANOTHER WEDDING, ANOTHER Sutherland sister marrying a damn Cavallo brother. Irritated, Dana Roux looked around her. Surely there were other sexy, gorgeous, sexy, to-die-for hunks around? Damn, she'd listed *sexy* twice.

Her best friend, Caitlin Sutherland, had married hotel tycoon Don Cavallo at the beginning of the year. Caitlin's sister Zoe had married Dale, Don's brother, during a ceremony on the tiny beach in Hermanus a week ago, but tonight the wedding party was being held here on Mahé, the biggest island of the Seychelles.

Dana realized she was scowling and tried to smile. But she wasn't sure it was working. If David flippin' Cavallo would just stop staring at her, she might start to enjoy the evening. Ever since she'd met the third Cavallo brother more than a year ago, he'd been a thorn in her hide, irritating her with his constant flirting.

She grabbed her bag. Maybe if she could escape for a few minutes, he would find someone else to stare at.

"I'm going to the ladies' room," she said to Hannah, who was sitting next to her, the only Sutherland sister not wrapped around a Cavallo brother.

"I'll join you," Hannah said, a grateful expression on her face, and they both got up.

The next minute the band started playing a slow dance and before Dana could move, David was standing in front of her. He held out his hand, a challenge in his eyes. "Dance?"

A quiver slid along her spine. Damn it to hell—why did his voice always have the same effect on her, melting her bones with just one word?

She wanted to refuse, wanted to turn around and flee as far away as possible from this party, but then she looked up and saw the knowing look in David's eyes. He knew, damn it. He knew exactly how uncomfortable he made her, and he knew she didn't want him touching her.

Steeling herself against the onslaught on her senses that was coming, she lifted her chin and placed her hand in his. He smiled, closed his hand around hers and, bringing their clasped hands up, let her twirl before he pulled her close.

And then, as she'd known would happen, sensation after sensation flooded her body—delicious shivers glided down her back, blood rushed through her veins, her heartbeat quickened, goose bumps covered her arms.

His nearness was overwhelming and did something to her, as she had discovered not so long ago when she'd danced with him during Caitlin and Don's wedding.

Like his three brothers, David was tall, dark, and breath-takingly handsome. And like any other red-blooded female, she noticed and enjoyed looking at them.

But ever since she'd laid eyes on David for the first time, he'd managed to rub her the wrong way. Oh, hell, not rub— she had to think of another word. Rub had connotations of bodies close to one another, of intimacy, and just thinking of her body close to David's...

She was carrying way too much baggage at the moment, baggage she wasn't sure she'd ever be able to let go, baggage she'd been constantly dealing with over the past two years. Ever since every newspaper in the country had featured her father's incarceration and subsequent suicide two years ago, she'd steered clear of any kind of relationship with the opposite sex.

The fact David used to be an investigative journalist put him in the category of stay-as-far-away-as-possible. True, he wasn't a journalist any longer, but he would probably know all there was to know about her dad's alleged involvement in a Ponzi scheme. As she'd gathered during numerous Sutherland get-togethers David had also attended, he was still very much interested in news that made headlines.

"Relax, Dana. It's a wedding; you're way too tense," David said and rubbed her shoulders.

Relax around David Cavallo? Not likely.

The last thing she wanted was for him to find out anything more about her life. He had this way of looking straight into her very being, as if he could read her mind, and she didn't like that. On the night she'd met him, she'd told herself to ignore the instant attraction. She'd told herself a thousand times he was way too attractive for his own good and not someone she wanted to get involved with. Trouble was, when she was this close to him, it was very difficult to remember her resolution.

Desperately, Dana looked around them, hoping to catch someone's eye who could interrupt the dance. But everyone else seemed to be having a good time. Every single Sutherland sister was staring up at a Cavallo brother, and their lively romance-writing mother was looking on, beaming.

How long can one dance be? The music seemed to go on forever. David was a wonderful dancer, but she didn't want to be this close to him, didn't want to be so aware of the heat his body was radiating, of the hard muscles underneath her fingers, of his intoxicating, all-David smell.

She closed her eyes, hoping to find some kind of balance, but with her eyes closed, her other senses only became more sensitive, picking up the hitch in his breath, the erratic beating of his heart, the warmth of his hands on her naked lower back.

He pulled her closer and steered her toward the big doors that led onto a wide veranda overlooking the beach. She stiffened but noticed other couples were also dancing out there and she relaxed. Slightly.

"It's a beautiful night." David's voice rumbled close to her ear.

The man had a voice that could melt steel.

How was a mere woman supposed to stay immune?

She nodded, realizing some kind of reaction was called for. At this point, she didn't think talking would be a good idea. Her mouth was dry, her brain muddled. She was incapable of saying anything, let alone stringing a coherent sentence together.

And he was right. It was a beautiful night. Decembers were hot in the Seychelles; it was the height of the tourist season. Of course, if someone was one of the owners, getting the venue at the biggest hotel for their wedding during high season on short notice was no problem.

She sighed. She was glad for both Caitlin and Zoe; that they'd found someone they loved. Really. From what she could see, both Don and Dale were smitten with their beautiful wives. So she was happy for them. But that didn't mean she had to play nice with David Cavallo every time there was a family thing going on.

It was, of course, possible to not accept an invitation to any of the family get-togethers but, because of her strained relationship with her mother, Dana had spent most of her high school years over at the Sutherland house. Over the course of time, she'd become part of the family. So much so, she was always invited to a family gathering. To start refusing invitations at this point would mean trying to explain something she herself wasn't quite sure about.

"Dana?" David stopped dancing. He pulled her to the side so they were standing behind one of the huge pillars.

"What?" she asked warily.

"I'm dancing with you, that's all. Do you have to look so ticked off about it?" He was still smiling, damn him.

"I'm not ticked off, it's just…"

He lifted his hand, and she forgot what she wanted to say.

Slowly, carefully, he combed his fingers through her hair.

Breathing became impossible.

"You're beautiful. Have I mentioned that before?" His whispered words were accompanied by his usual devastating smile.

Dumbstruck, she looked up at him. That David Cavallo might think she was beautiful had never occurred to her. There was seldom a newspaper or magazine that didn't carry a picture of one of the Cavallo men with a gorgeous woman at his side. David was no exception. She didn't have time to worry about her looks, but compared to the beauties he'd been photographed with, she was a plain Jane.

"You don't want to talk?" He smiled and lowered his head. "Well, that's fine, because talking is not what I have in mind when I'm around you."

And then he cupped her face with his hands and his lips claimed hers. She didn't expect that, wasn't ready for the sheer pleasure that streaked through her body, for the way her whole being responded to the simple action. Except being kissed by David was not simple. At all.

He lifted his head a fraction, still smiling lazily. Oh, so

for him this was just something to while away the time. He'd gotten her all hot and bothered while he was apparently unaffected by the kiss. Well, they would have to see about that. She was not going to be the only one having steamy dreams tonight.

Without taking her eyes off his, she moved her hands slowly over his muscled torso. His smile slipped, his heart tripped under her fingers, and she grinned. Two could play this game.

She crept one hand around his neck, and she brought his head down. Just before their lips met, she cocked her head and bit his lower lip softly between her teeth.

A growl erupted from within his throat, but before she could chuckle triumphantly, he turned the tables and pinned her against the pillar. He moved his knee between her legs and skimmed her sides with his hands before his lips devoured hers. Everything else around them ceased to exist.

Desperately she tried to cling to reality, tried to remember this was David Cavallo. He would know all there was to know about her dad's sordid story, but his arms closed around her and then nothing else seemed important anymore.

She sank into a stream of emotion, of feeling, where only her senses ruled. Every single rational thought left her mind and, resignedly, she stopped fighting the inevitable. Nothing could ever come of this; there would be no happily ever after like Caitlin and Zoe had, but Dana had this moment and she was going to enjoy it.

DAVID WAS DROWNING—HE couldn't get enough oxygen into his lungs. What the hell happened?

Kissing Dana Roux had seemed like a nice idea a few minutes ago, but *nice* was certainly not the right word to describe what he was feeling. Something very primitive, something he'd never experienced before, had taken over his usually analytical mind.

As a trained journalist, he was used to relying on this skill. Although he'd said goodbye to that career a while ago now, the skill he'd trusted to gather facts, to come to rational conclusions, had never before deserted him. But, hell, there was no analytical way to explain what Dana's warm body wrapped around his was doing to him, and the only conclusion that made sense was to get a room with a big bed as soon as possible.

A minute ago, he'd been in charge, putting the moves on Caitlin's friend. After all, flirting with beautiful women was part of his daily life. It was kind of expected of him, especially now that two of his brothers were married. And he'd always thought Dana was stunning. She, on the other hand, made no secret of the fact that he irritated her to no end.

It had been a first for him. Women usually responded to his flirtations, to his smile. But not this blonde. As Caitlin's best friend, she was usually around when his family and the

Sutherlands got together. He'd never really asked why, but Dana seemed to be a fixed part of the Sutherland clan, and she was always invited.

Trying to get her to at least acknowledge his existence had become a challenge. And he was always up for one. So he had made a point of flirting with her whenever they met just to get a rise out of her. And she always reacted so predictably.

Until tonight, that is. Because tonight he'd apparently pushed buttons he probably should have left alone.

One second he'd been merely enjoying an easy kiss, but then she'd used her teeth on his lower lip, and easy changed to complicated within those sexy seconds. He was hard for this woman. He wanted her with a need so passionate it was scaring the living daylights out of him.

Someone laughed out loud close to him, and he lifted his head, gulping in some much needed fresh air. Dana looked stunned. The dazed expression on her face mirrored his feelings.

"Dana, I—" he began, but she shook her head and moved away quickly.

"Please don't say anything." She combed her fingers through her hair. They weren't quite steady. "I agree, this was a huge mistake," she said and gestured wildly. "Let's blame the wine, the music, the night, whatever. You probably didn't even know it was me you were kissing. Forget about it—I already have." She tried a smile before she turned away.

For a millisecond, he was stunned, but he grabbed her arm and pulled her away from the other people before she could complete her turn.

His fingers closed around her upper arms, and he tugged her close to him. Close enough for her to know exactly how wrong she'd been. Her eyes widened; her mouth dropped open.

"Oh, I know who I was kissing." He hissed and pulled the lower part of her body close to his. "This," he said, making sure she could feel his hard-on, "is all you, Dana. Every throbbing, aching centimeter. You want to forget about this? Great. Let me know how you're doing." He growled and he swooped his head down before she could move away.

By now, he knew what she tasted like, knew how sweet and seductive her mouth was, and his lips covered hers hungrily. He swallowed her soft moan as her scent surrounded him. He allowed his hands to roam over her body, to journey over every curve and line, to revel in her softness here and in her toned feminine muscles there, until he closed his hand over one of her full breasts.

He nearly lost it then. He was a boob man; he'd always loved a woman's curves, loved the softness, the feel. Hell, what was not to love? But Dana's breasts were something entirely else. These were Nirvana, paradise. For these breasts he'd crawl over hot coals, walk over broken glass.

"David," Dana mumbled against his lips, but he didn't want to listen, didn't want anything else intruding in this glorious moment. She pushed against his shoulders again, and he lifted his mouth reluctantly.

"Calling," she panted. "Someone is calling you," she said, and he finally registered where they were.

Dazed, he looked around him before he turned back to Dana. She was muttering while pulling at her dress, her cheeks flaming.

"David!" Don's voice sounded close by, and he quickly stepped away from Dana and walked to the end of the wide veranda. He was in no state yet to talk to anyone else.

"Have you seen David?" He heard Don's voice again, closer this time. "Dale and Zoe are leaving."

"He's over there," Dana said softly, and David turned around in time to see her slipping past his brother and disappearing into the crowd.

Chapter Two

B Y THE TIME they'd said their farewells to the married couple, Dana's body had finally stopped humming. She was standing at the edge of the crowd, trying to make sure she was as far away from David as possible. Standing here, away from her friends, also gave her the opportunity to slip away unnoticed.

She still couldn't believe she'd kissed David with so much abandon. Even worse, that she did something she'd never done before—bit his lip, looking for some kind of reaction from him! And boy, oh boy, did she get a reaction.

With a last wave to the departing couple, she turned away, her only intention to get to her room as soon as possible.

Hannah caught her arm though. "Where are you off to? Please don't leave me alone with all these happy smiling couples—I'm not going to make it!" she wailed.

"I have an early flight tomorrow morning."

"But I thought you said it was school holiday at the moment? Why not stay in the Seychelles?"

"I wish I could but... um... there are other things..."

"Hannah, sweetheart!" Hannah's mother called out and grabbed her daughter's hand. "There is someone you have to meet." And pulling a frowning Hannah behind her, she disappeared among the other guests.

Dana sighed in relief and quickly glanced around her. Great, David was nowhere in sight. Hurrying forward, she pushed through the throng of people. She had to get to her room before he found her again. With everything that was on her mind, the last thing she needed was to be distracted by flutterings she didn't know how to deal with.

For the past two years, ever since her dad's suicide, she'd been trying to get to the truth of what had really happened. Her brother, George, an engineer, was working and living in Dubai, and it didn't look as if he'd be back in South Africa anytime soon. He'd been home for their dad's funeral, and her mother had been over to visit him last Christmas, but he had informed her in no uncertain terms that he didn't want to have anything to do with the whole mess. The sooner he could put the whole thing behind him, the better.

For her, it wasn't that easy. In spite of what the papers said and what she knew other people were thinking, she believed her dad to be innocent and she wanted to prove it.

"Dana!" Caitlin called from close by.

Dana groaned softly, as she'd nearly reached the elevators. She pasted a smile on her face and turned. "I thought you guys had left."

"We have a babysitter." Caitlin smiled. "The first time

since Donato's birth, and I, for one, am going to enjoy a little bit more of the night. Where are you off to in such a hurry?"

"I'm leaving in the morning…"

Caitlin took her hand and pulled her to one side. "We haven't had a chance to talk much over the past few months. How are you doing? Any news about what happened to your dad?"

"I have some leads and I want to use the holidays to see what I can find out."

"You will tell me if you need help?"

Dana sighed. "I know it's probably a useless battle but even after two years, I cannot accept that my dad would have knowingly been involved in a Ponzi scheme, that he committed fraud, took money from his clients, and didn't invest it through the proper channels. And, of course, I keep thinking if I could have gotten him out on bail, he would still be alive."

Caitlin gave her a hug. "And you're trying to prove he didn't commit suicide."

"Everyone keeps telling me there is no other explanation, but I know him. He would never have done anything to harm his family. I firmly believe that."

"And your mother isn't making your life any easier." Caitlin grimaced. "I know she's your mother, but really, the way she's treating you in spite of everything you do for her makes me so mad."

"Her world collapsed when my dad died." Dana shrugged.

She loved her mother but had never really understood her. Dana had long ago accepted the fact her mother didn't know what to do with a little girl. George was the oldest, the one her mother wanted, but Dana wasn't planned, a fact she'd heard often enough.

And now the irony of the whole situation was that her mom was dependent on Dana. And she tried to keep her happy, tried to provide for her every need, but on a teacher's salary that wasn't easy. There had been a life insurance policy, but according to her mother, it was not enough for her to live on.

"You can't continue to give in to her every demand, Dana. It must be so exhausting."

Dana shrugged and smiled. "Fortunately, your mother is close by—she has been a wonderful friend. Ever since you and I became friends at school, your mom has been my mom as well. She was the one who urged me to find out what really happened with my dad. Without all of your support, it would have been much more difficult to cope."

"Do you have any leads at this point?"

"I do. Well, I hope so. It's taken me two years but I've finally managed to track down one of the journalists who worked on the story, and I have an appointment to see him on my return. He was apparently not the one who wrote the story, but I'm hoping he can put me in touch with his colleague."

"Please remember we want to help, okay? But enough of all this gloom. Let's have a drink."

"I really wish I could, but I have an early flight tomorrow."

Caitlin frowned. "I know you said you were leaving, but I thought you'd take a later flight."

"Who's taking a flight?" Don asked coming up behind Caitlin and putting his arms around her.

Caitlin beamed and lifted her face for a kiss from her husband. Dana swallowed the sudden lump in her throat. These two obviously loved each other to bits. She was so glad for her friend but had made peace with the fact that such bliss was meant only for a chosen few people, and clearly Dana wasn't one of them.

"Dana is leaving early tomorrow morning," Caitlin complained. "I thought we'd still have a few hours together tomorrow. We're only leaving on Wednesday. You should have stayed until then."

"I have to get back," Dana said.

"Why don't you go with David?" Don asked. "He's leaving for Cape Town just before lunch on the company plane. No one else is going back so soon, so there is definitely a seat for you. Let me check with him." He smiled, and before Dana could say anything, he was beckoning David over.

It was one of those times she wished the floor would open up so she could disappear.

"You guys have paid for my plane ticket. It's not necessary—" she tried, but David was already strolling toward them.

"Of course we did," Caitlin said. "You were still teaching and couldn't fly out with us when we came."

Dana tried to duck behind one of the people in the crowd.

"Are you still the only passenger on the plane tomorrow?" Don asked David.

Dana hissed. "Don, really, I'm totally fine. I have a ticket and—"

"Yes," David said. "Who else needs a ride?"

"Dana here." Don pulled her closer.

David's eyes narrowed slightly.

"I have the plane ticket you've paid for, and I'm leaving early," Dana said nearly desperately. "I don't—"

"Oh, but you do." David took her hand. "What kind of a friend would I be if I didn't offer you a seat on our plane? If I'd known you were leaving, I would have suggested it myself."

There was a glint in his eyes she didn't trust, but short of throwing a tantrum, there wasn't much she could do. He let go of her hand slowly.

Caitlin clapped her hands together. "Great! Now we can have another glass of wine before you need to go to bed." She smiled and grabbed Dana's hand. "Let's go find a bottle of wine. We haven't had time for a chat in ages."

DAVID STARED AFTER the two beautiful women, his body still not quite back to normal. He couldn't remember the last time a woman had him all hot and bothered and aching for more. Much, much more.

Don slapped him on the back, bringing him back to earth. "She's beautiful, isn't she?" His brother smiled, also staring after the two women.

"Very beautiful," David murmured.

"Hey, you're talking about my wife!" Don growled and punched him on the shoulder.

"I wasn't talking about Caitlin." David immediately wished he could press a delete button to erase his words. He was never going to live this down.

Don laughed and grabbed their other brother's arm as he walked past them. "You should hear what our brother has to say about Dana Roux," he teased.

Darryn grimaced. "Please don't tell me another one of my brothers is about to become starry-eyed over a woman. It's becoming very boring around the lot of you."

"I said she's beautiful; I'm not starry-eyed. Besides, she made it abundantly clear she doesn't like me."

Don sobered. "It's probably because she knows you used to be a journalist."

Surprised, David looked at his brother. "Why? What does that have to do with anything?"

Don frowned. "I thought you knew. Because of what

happened to her dad. He was believed to have been involved with some Ponzi scheme in which thousands of people lost their money. The Bob Hastings mess? Surely you remember the case? He was the mastermind behind the whole thing. You were still working as an investigative journalist at the time. It was a big scandal and front-page news in all the newspapers, including the one you worked for. The article was the reason her dad was taken into custody."

David grimaced and nodded. How would he ever forget?

Don continued. "It was suggested that Dana's dad was working with the Hastings fellow. But exactly how deeply he was involved in the whole scheme is anyone's guess. He was arrested but committed suicide before he could testify. The mother, who sounds to me like she was difficult to begin with, fell apart after the whole incident and is making Dana's life a living hell. Not that she's complaining, but the fact she spends more time at the Sutherland house than with her mother should tell you something."

David stared at his brother. His brain was finally linking the dots. Roux. "You mean her dad was Gareth Roux?" he asked his brother.

Don nodded. "Yeah, that's the name." Don cocked his head. "Come to think of it, wasn't it your story?"

David swore. "Yes, it was my story. It was also the story that made me quit the job and join you guys. The best decision I've ever made."

Darryn frowned. "I remember you were upset about a

story, but I didn't know it was about Dana's dad."

"I was more than upset. I got a tip that Bob Hastings's business might not be all it was supposed to be, heard something here and there, and told the editor about the rumors that were going around. At that point, I didn't have all the facts; I was still checking and double-checking everything, but I wanted to let him know what I was working on. I still needed another couple of days to talk to people, especially about Gareth Roux's involvement. I wasn't so sure he knew what was going on, but the editor smelled money and went ahead and printed what I had. And even though he didn't use my name in the byline, everybody at the paper knew it was my story. I was livid. But it was too late. I realized then that the truth and ethics didn't matter; selling papers was and still is what counts. That's when I quit."

He rubbed his hand over his face. "And after a few days, Dana's dad was dead," he murmured, still recalling how angry and dismayed he'd been. Roux was a name he'd written in brackets on his notes; he hadn't even begun digging up facts about the man, but the editor had printed the man's name, and he had been questioned and taken into custody.

"Well, you had better tell her before you do more than drool over her." Don smiled.

David nodded, his head reeling. He'd, of course, heard Dana's surname before. It was a common enough surname, but it had never even crossed his mind that the man who still haunted his dreams was also her dad. He stopped investigating after he'd decided to quit his job, but the case had been bothering him all this time.

At least he now knew why he was never included in Dana's smile. His crime was that he'd been a journalist. And if she knew he was the one responsible for everything that had happened to her dad, he would probably never see her again.

Don was right. Tomorrow, they would be spending a six-hour flight together, during which time he'd have to tell her he was the one who had spilled the story. It wasn't something he was looking forward to, but at least then she'd have a definite reason not to like him. And he'd do it because it was the right thing to do, not because he was drooling over her. Was he?

He grabbed another glass of wine from a passing waiter. All he'd thought of when Don asked him if Dana could fly with him tomorrow was how interesting things could become in the small space of their aircraft. He downed the wine. Now he wished he could think up an excuse not to have to fly with her.

Not because he didn't want to. After what had happened between the two of them tonight, there was nothing he'd like better than to explore what else lay hidden behind Dana's cool exterior. But the whole thing had just become way beyond complicated.

There was a moment earlier tonight when she'd been in his arms, and he'd felt something so intense, so real, he'd forgotten to think, to analyze, to explain. And truth be told, he was a little bit freaked out. So maybe it wasn't such a bad idea to tell her about his role in the whole scandal. That would surely be reason enough for her to resent him for the rest of his life. And, at the moment, that seemed like the saner option.

It would be much better if she hated him, ignored him. Life would resume its normal, boring pace, and all would be well with his heart.

Why, then, was he still looking for her? Swearing, he turned and headed in the direction of his room.

Chapter Three

S HE'D RUN OUT of excuses last night. Caitlin had an answer for everything she'd tried to suggest to get out of flying back to South Africa with David Cavallo.

Dana braced herself and walked toward the small plane where David was waiting for her. Oh, my goodness, just look at him! The blatant maleness of the man simply took her breath away.

For a minute, she was worried her knees would give way beneath her, but somehow, she made it all the way to the steps leading up to the plane where he was waiting.

Strangely enough, this morning there wasn't a mocking smile to contend with. He was hiding behind his sunglasses and looked grim. With a nod, he took her arm and helped her up the steps.

The touch of his hand on her skin nearly had her tripping over her own feet, but he put an arm around her to help her up the last few steps. The pilot came out of the cockpit, and he and David started talking. A flight attendant showed her to a comfortable seat and offered her a glass of sparkling wine.

Wow. The rich sure did things on a grander scale than what she was used to. She shook her head and looked out the window. Wine would only muddle up the last shreds of rational thought she was valiantly trying to hold on to.

She'd hardly slept a wink last night. The whole kissing scene kept her up most of the night. And when she hadn't been berating herself for throwing herself at David, she remembered every sensory sensation that had raced through her body.

Why she couldn't get the whole thing out of her head was beyond her. Yes, it had been a good kiss and, okay, she hadn't been kissed in quite some time, but it wasn't as if she'd never locked lips with a man before. Yet somehow David's kiss had managed to wipe away the memory of every other meeting of lips she'd had before. It was as if he was the only guy she'd ever kissed!

She closed her eyes. The last things she should be thinking about were kissing and David Cavallo.

She was about to spend the next six or so hours in close proximity with him. Very close even for a luxurious plane.

She opened her eyes and there he was, taking his seat directly opposite her. A groan threatened to escape and she swallowed. How was she supposed to act normally when this hot guy who'd been kissing her a few hours ago was sitting so close to her?

She grabbed her bag and started rummaging through it. Somewhere she had a book.

Caitlin's mother wrote love stories and had introduced Dana to the wonders of happy endings when she'd been a young sixteen. And, to this day, when things got a bit more than she could handle, she would escape to a fictional world where everyone was happy in the end. And right now seemed to be a perfect time to escape a different reality.

Even if she didn't take in anything she read, she'd at least have something else to look at besides David Cavallo.

WHEN DANA OPENED a book, David pulled his laptop closer and tried to concentrate. There was a lot of work that needed his attention at the moment, and normally he'd use the time on a plane to catch up on e-mails.

But one look at Dana this morning had left him nearly drooling. She was wearing a pair of jeans and a T-shirt, nothing he hadn't seen on women before. But on Dana the ordinary T-shirt curved lovingly around her generous breasts and the skinny jeans reminded him vividly how her warm body had felt against his last night.

Speaking to the pilot just now had forced him to think of other matters, but now that he was sitting opposite Dana, his body had taken over his brain again, and his pants were feeling tighter by the minute.

He looked up to find her gaze on him. She quickly glanced down at her book again. He stared at her a minute longer. Swallowing a grin, he moved forward and took the book from her hands, turned it over, and handed it back.

"It would be easier to read it right side up, I think," he said solemnly.

She stared at him for a minute before she giggled and hid her face behind the book.

The giggle went right down to his groin and, in one movement, he put his laptop down and took the seat next to Dana.

She gasped. "What are you doing?"

He took the book from her limp fingers and threw it on the opposite seat.

"You weren't reading."

She shook her head. "You weren't working."

He shook his head. They stared at each other.

"David," she began and tried to move away, but he leaned forward and put his hand behind her head.

"I have to talk to you, but first... I have to taste you again. I have to see whether I remember correctly," he muttered before his lips claimed hers.

SENSATIONS SLAMMED INTO her, raced through her body, and all she could do was cling to David. His broad shoulders were a hard rock underneath her fingers while his mouth was devouring hers.

This had to stop; she shouldn't be kissing David Cavallo. The plane hadn't even taken off yet, and she was already plastered against him. She pushed against him, hoping he would stop, but he deepened the kiss, and she was lost.

"I'm sorry, sir," a voice said somewhere above them, and David lifted his head. His brown eyes were smoldering, his breathing erratic.

"Yes?" Without taking his hands from Dana, he looked up at the flight attendant.

"You should fasten your seat belts; we're about to take off," she said with a smile.

Dana put her hands against her burning cheeks. What was she thinking? Embarrassed, she fidgeted, looking for the seat belts, until David covered her hand with his. Silently he put the seat belt around her body, his fingers lightly grazing her hard nipples.

His nostrils flared and she stopped breathing.

Unable to look away, she stared at him while he fastened his seat belt.

The plane gathered speed and she closed her eyes. David covered her hand with his again, and he entwined his fingers with hers.

She was not supposed to sit here and allow him to kiss her, to touch her! Whatever this sudden flaring up of hormones between the two of them was, it had to stop. She tried pulling her hand from underneath his, but his fingers simply folded her hand completely in his, and she stopped fidgeting.

For the few minutes it took for the plane to reach the desired altitude, she sat quietly, acutely aware of his hand around hers, of his scent slowly penetrating through every pore of her skin until it became part of her breathing, her heartbeat. His body radiated heat, heat that was muddling her brain, making her forget all the reasons she shouldn't get involved with this man. Ever.

When they were finally in the air, she pulled her hand away and loosened her seat belt. This time when the flight attendant offered her a glass of champagne, she didn't hesitate to take it. She tried to move slightly away from David's overwhelming presence.

He also took a glass and held it out to her. "To... the interesting things that happen at weddings." There was a teasing light in his eyes.

"David, please... let's forget about last night. It should never have happened. I don't even like you!" Her frustration with the whole situation boiled over.

"Why is that?" David asked mildly and put his glass down.

Realizing she'd said too much, she shook her head and took another sip of champagne.

David took her glass from her and put it next to his. "Would it help if I tell you I know you don't like me because I used to be a journalist?"

She whipped her head around and stared at him. "So you know about my dad?" she asked trying to look calm.

He nodded but before he could say anything else, his phone rang. Without taking his eyes off hers, he answered his phone. But whoever was talking to him got his attention, and he stood up and walked away.

Dana breathed freely for the first time since he'd sat next to her. There never seemed to be enough oxygen in the air when she was close to him.

She stared at his back, noticed the way his T-shirt clung to his broad shoulders, the way his jeans fitted snugly around his very sexy behind.

Swallowing a groan, she closed her eyes, remembering vividly his pulsing body as he'd made her aware of his desire for her last night.

Damn it. What the hell was going on? She'd dated guys before, gorgeous guys, hot guys, sexy guys. But at the moment, she couldn't recall any of their faces.

She'd seen David several times before—she'd danced with him at Don and Caitlin's wedding. And even though her heart always went a little crazy when she was near him, although her mouth became dry, and her blood heated instantly, she'd managed to ignore her body's antics and play it cool. Until last night, that was. Until he'd kissed her, until he'd shown her how his own body reacted after their kiss.

Whether she wanted to admit it or not, his kiss had touched something inside of her, touched her very core. As a biology teacher, she knew it was probably just her dopamine levels causing the havoc in her body, but her heart wasn't listening. Oh, no, her heart was on its own mission, merrily jumping about inside her body at the mere thought that

David would be back any minute now.

And then he came strolling back. But instead of taking the seat next to her, he grabbed his laptop and moved to another row of seats altogether.

"There seems to be a problem with our website. The technical guys have fixed it, but I need to add the rest. And it can't wait." He opened his mouth, obviously changed his mind, and closed it again before he sat down.

"I want to talk to you about your dad and what happened, but I have to sort this out first."

Dana nodded and opened her book again, this time with the right side up. It was for the best anyway. She didn't want to talk to him, she didn't want to talk about her dad, and she definitely didn't want to talk to him about her dad. Somehow, she needed to make sure she stayed as far away from him as possible.

From now on, she would find excuses not to attend the Sutherland and Cavallo gatherings. At least until these foolish feelings had vanished.

Finding a way to tell Caitlin she would not be attending all the family get-togethers from now on without alerting her friend to the fact that she had the hots for her brother-in-law would be tricky, but surely Dana could come up with a good enough reason?

Exasperated with herself, Dana slowly reread the first line of the story. She couldn't believe what she was thinking! Having the hots for David Cavallo was not what should be happening; her life was complicated enough already.

She glanced up. David was staring at his computer, a frown carved into his forehead. Her eyes trailed over his face, down his muscled upper body, and she had to force her gaze down to the book.

Every fiber of her being was aware of the man sitting a few meters away from her.

For the umpteenth time, she reread the first few lines of the book. Maybe if she had a gory thriller to read, she would have been able to forget about the man sitting nearby. A love story where the hero was described as sexy as sin was way too close a description of the situation with the real flesh-and-blood man sitting near her.

Chapter Four

DAVID SWORE UNDER his breath. Normally, this would have taken him only minutes to finish. But with Dana close by, he had a hard time trying to focus on what had to be done. And he'd just become aware she was looking at him. That wasn't helping his concentration.

He looked up. She was reading again. Or at least she was looking down at the book. Whether she was actually taking in anything was another matter altogether. She shifted and dropped the book onto her lap. The thin T-shirt revealed she was either cold or…

Groaning softly, he raked his hands through his hair. He wanted to throw his computer away, lock everyone else in the cockpit, and take Dana to the big bed tucked away in the corner so he could put his hands on her in every way he'd imagined. He wanted her, and this craving was driving him insane.

He willed his body to behave and forced his attention back to his computer. He and Darryn were responsible for the advertising and marketing of the hotel group he and his brothers owned. Darryn used to be a photographer, and part of his job still entailed taking photographs. David did all the copywriting for the ads, and between the two of them they had to make sure everyone knew about their hotels.

If he didn't fix this problem now, his brothers would not be too happy with him. A glance in Dana's direction showed him she had slid down in the seat and closed her eyes. Good. A sleeping Dana he could handle. It was the wide-awake one that was giving him problems.

As he stared, she rolled onto her side, and the T-shirt moved up to reveal a tiny part of her golden skin. Swearing softly, he grabbed his computer and moved to the seats farthest from her. What the hell? He had work to finish, damn it. He didn't have time to sit and drool over a bloody woman.

DANA STOPPED BREATHING in anticipation.

David's fingers found their way underneath her T-shirt and he slipped his hands higher and higher. Wantonly she moved closer to him so she could give him better access...

"Dana! Dana!"

He was calling out her name. She frowned. But why was he doing it so loudly? She opened her eyes and there he was. David. For a minute she stared up at him, until she heard the other voices behind him and realized they had landed. She'd been dreaming, and his hands weren't under her T-shirt.

She sat up quickly and looked at her watch. Oh, hell,

she'd slept the whole time, undoubtedly because she'd hardly slept the night before. Quickly she combed her fingers through her hair and got up. Her makeup was probably smudged, her hair a tangled mess.

"I'm sorry, I must look terrible. I didn't think I would sleep this long…" she started babbling, but David took her hand and she stopped speaking.

"You look beautiful." His eyes darkened and he kissed her.

Before her befuddled brain could construe a sentence, he ran his fingers through her hair.

"I want to talk to you, but I can't now, and I won't be able to come to Hermanus before the weekend. Can I see you then?"

She opened her mouth to say no, but someone called him and he moved away. The very last thing she wanted to do was to make a date with this man who had been occupying her mind every waking and sleeping moment for the last few hours. It was ridiculous to feel this way, to react this way to his presence. Nothing could ever come of it; she knew that.

The flight attendant opened the door of the plane and showed Dana out. Before she could descend the stairs, David was there, his arm held protectively around her. His phone rang, and he talked to someone until they entered what looked like a VIP lounge.

Dana looked around, trying to orient herself. Two days

ago, she'd driven to the airport with her own car and had parked it in one of the parking garages. It was an expense she couldn't really afford, but in the end it was much cheaper than a shuttle service from and to Hermanus. And asking her mother was not an option.

Dana spotted her luggage near the door and grabbed her bag. David was still on his phone, and she motioned to the flight attendant that she was leaving. Quickly, she slipped past the milling people, her only thought to get away quickly.

THE CLIENT FINALLY ran out of things to say and David was able to end the call. Irritated, he put his cell phone in his pocket. Some people simply talked way too much. But Gary was one of their biggest clients and David had to stay nice.

He turned around, expecting to see Dana behind him. But she was nowhere to be seen.

"Where is Dana?" he asked the flight attendant, who was hovering close by.

"She's left," she said and pointed toward the door leading into the airport building.

Swearing, David stormed out, his gaze combing the crowd. Why the hell hadn't she waited for him? And how was she getting to Hermanus? He never got around to asking her.

Just when he thought he'd missed her, he spotted the

blonde with the long legs leaving the airport building. She'd put her hair up in a ponytail, but he'd know that walk, that sexy sway of the hips, anywhere. He sprinted and ducked, never taking his eyes off her swinging ponytail.

She was standing in front of a parking machine, opening her purse, when he finally caught up with her.

"Dana," he called out, and she turned her head.

"Why didn't you wait for me?" he asked, taking the parking ticket from her hand.

She made a grab for it, but he held on, taking out his own wallet.

"I want to leave and that's my ticket—I'm paying for it!" she snapped, still tugging on the ticket.

He grabbed her hands in his empty one and pulled her closer while he pushed the ticket into the machine.

"I want to do this for you."

Her eyes flashed. "I can pay for my own—"

"I know, but let me do this," he insisted and waited until she'd stopped fidgeting. Then he pulled out some bills and pushed them into the slot of the machine.

Dana stood by silently, her whole body radiating her displeasure.

The machine spat out the parking ticket, and he handed it over to her. She grabbed it out of his hand, turned on her heels, and strode toward the elevator. He followed but took her bag. She glared at him, opened her mouth to say something, but four other people entered the elevator and she fell silent.

When the elevator stopped on the level for the second parking bay, she tried to take her bag, but he refused to let it go, and with a huff she walked out.

He followed, becoming a little bit irritated with the whole scene. What was it with this woman? Most women wouldn't be offended if he offered to pay for something or if he tried to help them. In fact, paying for something was usually a sure way to get into their good books and into their beds, he'd learned.

She walked stiffly toward a small car that had obviously seen better days.

Dismayed, he stared at the car. Surely she wasn't planning on traveling in this piece of tin all the way to Hermanus?

"Don't you dare say a word about my car. Not all of us can afford the type of car you are used to," she snapped and opened the trunk of the car.

He lifted the bag into the trunk and closed the lid.

She walked quickly past him to the driver's door and opened it.

"Thank you for the plane ride, for paying for my parking ticket, for carrying my bag, although I would have been able to cope all on my own, like I have for the last ten years since I've been earning a salary." Clearly miffed, she turned to get into the car.

Before she could move, he pinned her to the car. They

stared at each other, both of them breathing hard.

"I was trying to help you," he snarled. "Usually women like that."

She narrowed her eyes and tried to break free from his hands. "I'm not most women."

"I know." He sighed, and just like that the irritation left his body. He slid his hands up her sides and he kissed her.

DANA OPENED HER mouth to protest, but David slid his tongue through her lips, and she forgot why she'd been so angry with him. Their tongues met, and his teased hers while he moved his hands restlessly up and down her sides.

There was so much heat, flames licking right beneath her skin. Was it possible to burst into flames? He folded his hands around her breasts, and she snaked her arms around his neck, pulling him closer to her.

Far away, cars were honking, people were laughing, but here within this cocoon where she and David were floating, nothing else could intrude, nothing else mattered.

And then he stepped between her legs, slid his hands beneath her T-shirt, just like in her dream, and explored her flesh, lighting small fires just below the surface of her skin wherever he touched her.

Any minute now he'd be touching her breast.

She strained upward, wantonly moving her body closer to his.

His phone rang, a car backfired and, cursing, David lifted his head.

Dana stared helplessly up at him. For the life of her, she couldn't remember why she'd been so angry with him, why she'd wanted to get away from him so urgently, why she hadn't wanted to be near him.

He looked down at his phone but didn't answer it. Instead, he switched it off and put it back in his pocket. He put his hands back on her shoulders, but reality came crashing down.

Dana ducked underneath his arm and slid into her car. She quickly closed the door and rolled down the window.

"Thank you for… everything."

"Everything?" he teased and leaned forward on the car with his arms.

"This"—she motioned her hand between them—"is ridiculous. You know it. I know it."

"I'll call you about the weekend."

She shook her head. "Not a good idea…"

"There's something I want to tell you about your father."

Irritated, she stared at him. She didn't want to see him again, but she wanted to hear what he had to say, and he knew it, damn it.

He lifted his hand and touched her face. "And we also have to talk about this thing between us."

"There is no thing…" she started heatedly, but he leaned in and kissed her.

A gasp escaped her lips before she could stop it.

He lifted his head, his eyes mere slits. "Really? Because your body says something entirely different." He lightly touched one of the protruding nipples straining against her T-shirt.

She inhaled sharply. "I—I... y-you..." she stuttered, unable to form a coherent sentence.

"I'll phone you." He stepped back.

Dana turned the key, praying fervently that her car would play along today.

It sputtered and made a few strange noises, but it started up eventually. Without looking at David again, she reversed and sped away. The man was making her behave in ways she'd never thought possible. Groaning out loud, she turned onto the national road that would take her all the way to Hermanus.

Christmas was a few weeks away, and the roads were busy. Holidaymakers were streaming down to visit all the seaside places for the summer holidays. She had to focus on the traffic. She couldn't be thinking about David's kisses, David's hands on her body.

The bloody man was too attractive for his own good. As one of the billionaire hotel tycoon brothers, he could have his pick of any beautiful woman out there. Why was he so intent on toying with her?

Because there was no way he could be seriously interested in her. She was an absolute nobody.

Okay, maybe he did know something about her dad that might help her investigation into the whole sorry mess. She'd listen to what he had to say about her father, but that was it. Whatever else he wanted, he'd have to find somewhere else.

Her body hadn't yet settled down after David's kisses and touch, but that she would have to ignore. How difficult could that be? She wasn't a schoolgirl anymore, damn it!

Chapter Five

D ANA STARED AT the journalist, not believing what she was hearing.

"David Cavallo?" she heard herself say from far away. She swallowed, trying to make sense of what she was hearing. "The David Cavallo who is now co-owner of a string of boutique hotels?" she asked, although she already knew the answer.

Sean Murray, the journalist she was talking to, nodded. "Yup, the same. Although, to be fair, he wasn't going to print the story before he'd…"

But Dana had stopped listening. A pain sliced through her body, making breathing difficult. She jumped up and frantically looked for the nearest exit. Why couldn't she breathe? Pushing past people, she kept her eyes on the door, her only thought to get away from here before she threw up or passed out—or both.

This was not what she'd expected when she'd made the appointment with this journalist. She'd thought hearing what he had to say might bring some sort of closure, give her some idea of exactly what role her father had played in the whole thing. But what she had learned was devastating.

David was the journalist who had run the front-page story that suggested her dad was involved in Bob Hastings's crooked financial scheme. The story that had led to her dad's incarceration.

Outside the coffee shop, she looked around helplessly. Where had she parked?

Hysterical laughter bubbled up inside of her. The man she'd allowed to kiss her, to touch her, the one she'd been dreaming and fantasizing about for the past five nights was the very same person who had been responsible for her dad's death.

She stumbled to her car through a haze of tears. He had been a journalist; she didn't want to get close to him for exactly that reason, but did she listen to her instincts? No. She'd let herself be seduced by a pair of chocolate-brown eyes and had forgotten to shelter her heart.

She turned the key. Her car coughed, stuttered, and died. Just like that.

"Please, don't do this to me. Please, please?"

Frantically, she tried again, but this time there wasn't even a cough.

Her phone rang. It was Caitlin. Taking deep breaths, she answered.

"Hi." She gulped in some air, trying to cover the hitch in her throat so Caitlin wouldn't know she'd been crying.

It was quiet for a heartbeat. "What's wrong?" Caitlin

asked, and the dam burst.

Dana tried to stem her tears, tried to speak, but all the pent-up emotions of the last two years had found an escape and wouldn't let up.

"Dana, sweetie, what happened?" Caitlin was clearly also upset.

Caitlin found a tissue, blew her nose, and tried again to speak.

"I… just spoke to the journalist… the one I told you about," she said, hiccupping.

"That's why I was phoning. What—"

"He told me the story on the cover, the one that got my dad arrested? It was David's story! I… can't believe he didn't tell me!" The tears were back. "And now my car won't start!"

"Where are you?" Caitlin asked.

"In Green Point. I met him at the coffee shop. But don't worry about me, I'll figure something out." She searched for her usual calm.

"I know you can do it all but let me help you. I'm on my way to the Waterfront and am very close to you. Sit tight, I'll be there in five." She ended the call.

Dana put her head on the steering wheel and let the tears flow. It wasn't the end of the world; she'd been in worse situations before, and she had always managed to handle things.

What had happened to her dad was devastating, but two years had passed, and she was getting used to the idea that she would never see him again. And she had known her car wasn't going to last; she'd been saving as much as she could and had been hoping she'd have a few more months before she needed to buy a new car. But she could do it now. It might not be the car she really wanted, but it would be okay.

So that wasn't why she was so distraught. She felt... betrayed somehow. Betrayed by David.

Betrayed because he had kissed her, touched something inside of her, made her feel special, and he hadn't told her he was the one who had spilled the story.

She had never even thought of asking him what he knew about the case. But then, they hadn't really talked much. Before the weekend she'd mostly tried to ignore him, and then at Zoe's wedding... Well, her lips were involved but not because she was talking.

She frowned. He did say he wanted to talk to her about her dad, but she'd assumed he wanted to tell her what she already knew.

It was probably all he would have done. The journalists she knew never took responsibility for what they'd written, they were only interested in what they could get out of it— the front-page story, the glory, the name.

A car turned into the parking space in front of her car. It was Caitlin. Dana grabbed her bag and got out quickly.

DAVID WAS STANDING with his back to the office door,

talking to one of their clients on the phone, his thoughts not on what his client was saying but on the weekend ahead. For the moment, he was alone in the big office his brothers and he normally shared.

He was going to Hermanus tomorrow. He was going to see Dana, and he couldn't wait. While he wasn't looking forward to telling her about his involvement with the story about her dad, hopefully he would be able to explain what had really happened.

Ever since Don had inherited a house from their uncle in Hermanus, the four of them tried to visit the beautiful seaside village regularly. He loved Hermanus, loved Walker Bay, especially this time of the year when the whales were visiting.

But, lately, there never seemed to be time to spend there. He enjoyed working with his brothers, enjoyed the challenges they faced every day, the adrenaline rush when deals were finalized, but he hadn't had a holiday in… Hell, he couldn't remember the last time he took a few days off.

He would have to talk to his brothers about having a few days to himself. Don took leave for a whole month when he got married, and Dale would also be gone for about a month with his new wife.

Well, he wasn't getting married, but he would like to be able to take a couple of weeks' leave.

He blinked. Married? He waited for the usual panicky feeling he got when he heard the word, and lately the word had been used a lot in his family, but he wasn't freaked out about it as he normally would have been.

Previously, the word would have called up images of husbands gasping for their freedom, hating their new lives, making crude jokes about wives and kids. But after two of his brothers had gotten hitched, although he would never willingly admit this to them, his usual grim view of matrimony was changing.

Both Don and Dale were better versions of themselves after they became involved with the loves of their lives. They were both besotted with their wives and didn't bother to hide the fact.

David liked women but had never met one who had stirred more than a mild interest. And he wanted more. Simply put, he wanted what his parents had.

After nearly forty years of marriage, the spark they said brought them together hadn't dimmed at all. Quite the contrary, actually. He loved the way his mom's face simply lit up when she spotted her husband, and he adored the way his dad always found ways to touch his mother.

And without conscious thought, ever since he'd started dating, he'd been looking for that spark, that moment when eyes would meet and he'd know. That feeling that he simply had to touch the woman. There had been sparks all right. He'd touched his share of women but nothing that lasted. Usually, after one night he couldn't wait to leave and the spark, or whatever it had been, was gone.

But then he'd kissed Dana Roux. When he'd seen her for the first time, he thought she was beautiful, and he was intrigued by her obvious dismissal of him, but that was it. He couldn't remember a spark, didn't remember his fingers tingling because they desperately wanted to touch her.

But after he kissed her, that had changed. He couldn't quite put his finger on it, but he couldn't stop thinking about the woman, and he wanted to be with her. He couldn't wait to touch her again, to feel her soft skin, to taste her lips, to—

The office door flew open. David turned around. Don strolled in, a mocking smile on his face.

"You're in trouble, my dear brother. To quote a line from one of my wife's favorite rom-com movies, 'the shit hath hitteth the fan.'" Don grinned and slapped David on the back.

"Why? What have I done?" David asked.

"Well, you remember the story about Hastings? About Dana's dad?"

Frowning, David nodded. "What about it?"

"Turns out Dana saw a journalist this morning who told her you were the one who spilled the beans. I thought you were going to tell her?"

David stared at Don, struggling to make sense of his words.

"I was going to tell her, but… she fell asleep," he ended lamely. He wasn't ready to talk about what had really happened. "Anyway, I'm planning on going to Hermanus this weekend, partly to tell her the whole story. Who did she talk to? Do you know?"

"Sean… something…"

"Sean Murray." David swore. "He could have told me he was discussing it with someone," he muttered. "Why was she talking to him?"

"I'm not quite sure."

"Where is she now?"

"It has been a bad morning for her. On top of hearing her friend's brother-in-law is the one who spilled the story about her dad, her car also broke down. Caitlin is going to take her back to Hermanus. They're just picking up Donato's stuff; he'll be staying with Mom until Caitlin gets back."

Before Don finished speaking, David grabbed his laptop and headed for the door. She had to listen to him. He ignored the elevator and stormed down the stairs, a feeling of desperation urging him to get to Dana as quickly as possible.

"I FEEL TERRIBLE that you have to drive all the way to Hermanus," Dana said softly while playing with Donato. Caitlin was packing a huge bag with Donato's things.

"Don's mom loves to have Donato. She spoils him rotten and is always glad to look after him. And we'll have time to catch up. Are you feeling better? I haven't seen you so upset since you got the news about your dad two years ago. Why were you talking to this guy?"

"You know I told you I've been trying to find out how involved my dad was in this whole Hastings business. I can't believe he knowingly did something illegal. I also find it difficult to believe he took his own life. It's just not who he was." She cuddled the baby close to her, inhaling his sweet baby smell. "Anyway, I've been asking around whenever I got the chance. The police were no help, and eventually I started contacting newspapers. This guy responded."

"What exactly did he say that upset you so much?" Caitlin asked.

"I told you. That David was the one who broke the story. He was the reason why my dad was taken in for questioning, ended up in the police cells where he was found dead hours later. That's why I'm upset. We spent six hours on a flight, and he kissed me but didn't think to tell me about what he'd done!"

Donato started whimpering. Damn, she'd spoken too loudly.

"Sorry, sweetie, sorry," she crooned and kissed the baby. Only then did she look at Caitlin, who had stopped packing and was looking astounded at her.

"What?"

"Rewind a bit," Caitlin instructed. "David kissed you?"

Belatedly, Dana realized what she'd said. "I... he... it wasn't a kiss, really... it was..." She trailed off and buried her flaming face in the baby's neck.

"Yeah? What was it then that makes you blush?" Caitlin teased and took Donato from her.

"We had too much to drink, it was a lovely night, I don't know! He... he's a Cavallo—they flirt. You know that!" Dana called out.

"Flirt? Yes. Kiss? Not every woman, no. So, tell me, when did David start kissing you?"

"He... I... it was only..." Dana stopped talking and pressed her hands against her warm cheeks.

"Yeah? That good?" Caitlin teased. "I didn't know you had a thing for my brother-in-law."

"I don't have a thing for him," Dana denied hotly. "I... we... just..."

"Kissed?" Caitlin giggled.

"I... the kiss is not the point," Dana insisted. "The point is, he should have told me about his part in the story." For the first time, she thought about something. "Did you know he was the one who wrote the story?"

Caitlin nodded. "But only since the weekend. Don told me after Zoe and Dale's wedding. It's not something David has spoken about before, but he told them about it that night." Caitlin hesitated. "I've never wanted to pester you with questions before, but can you explain to me what exactly a Ponzi scheme is?"

Dana nodded. "Believe me, I can. I've read just about everything about it I could put my hands on. It's a fraudulent investment operation where the operator, an individual or organization, pays returns to its investors from new capital paid to the operators by new investors, rather than from profit earned by the operator."

"Why Ponzi?" Caitlin asked.

"This type of scheme is named after Charles Ponzi who became notorious when he used the technique as far back as 1920." She grimaced. "The idea was actually described as far back as 1844 in Charles Dickens's novel, *Martin Chuzzlewit*, and also in *Little Dorrit* a few years later."

"And people still fall for it?" Caitlin asked, her eyes wide.

"The initial big returns on investments, unfortunately, still get the attention of anyone desperate to make money. Even though people are warned time and again, they still believe the scheme they put money into will be different. In this scheme, Hastings apparently told investors their money would buy buildings that would be renovated. And he did use some of the money for one or two buildings. But most of the money disappeared into his own pockets.

"But I know my dad would never knowingly become involved in a scheme like that, and I'd like to know why David thought my dad was involved."

"Wait until you've spoken to him. Don told me what really happened, but I'd rather David tell you the rest of the story himself. I don't know whether I have all the facts straight."

"I don't want to see him again!" Dana called out. "I feel… betrayed!"

Caitlin touched her hand. "Give him a chance to tell you his side of the story. I know David, and I know he'd never willingly do something to cause anyone harm. Besides"—she smiled mischievously and grabbed one of Dana's hands—"you did kiss the guy!"

"I didn't kiss him, he kissed me!"

Caitlin giggled. "Well, from experience, I know it's very difficult not to return a Cavallo kiss."

Dana wanted to stay angry, but her friend's giggle was infectious. "Okay, yeah, they know how to kiss," she agreed reluctantly. She sobered quickly. "But he should have told me. He did say he wanted to talk to me about it, but he never got around to it."

"Well, there you have it. He was probably going to tell you the story, but then he got sidetracked when he kissed you." Caitlin had a twinkle in her eye just as the front doorbell chimed. "That will be my mother-in-law. Wait till she hears about it," she teased and jogged toward the front door, her baby bobbing up and down in her arms.

Alarmed, Dana followed her. "Don't you dare say anything to her! She's going to tell your mother, and then I'll end up in one of her stories!"

"I know!" giggled Caitlin as she opened the door. "Isn't it wonderful!"

"What is so wonderful?" Don's mother stood smiling on the doorstep.

"David kissed Dana!" Caitlin sang, giving her mother-in-law a hug.

"It's about time. I was wondering when he'd get around to it." Rosa was still smiling as she entered the house.

Dana wished she could disappear into thin air.

But the older woman pulled her closer for a hug. "I knew it!" she whispered. "And I'm so pleased." Rosa took her arm, and they turned to walk toward the kitchen while Caitlin started closing the front door.

Dana tried to explain. "There is nothing going on, I promise you. It was just a kiss, just one... well, maybe two..."

"Three actually, but who's counting?" David said behind them, and Dana spun around.

He was standing on the doorstep where his mother had stood a few minutes ago. Her heart leaped up and bounced for joy.

Chapter Six

"D AVID!" HIS MOTHER held out her arms to him.
Without taking his eyes off Dana, he stepped into his mother's hug.

"Hi, David." Caitlin stood on tiptoes and kissed him. "It's nice to see you; is everything all right?"

"I don't know." His eyes were still on Dana. "I hope so. I heard about your interview with Sean Murray. Are you okay?"

Dana lifted her chin. "Am I okay?" she asked, putting enough incredulity in her voice to make him wince. "I can't believe you're asking me that. No, I'm not okay. I had to hear from a stranger that you were the one who put the story about my dad on the front page of a newspaper before you knew your facts." She rubbed a hand over her face. "And you didn't tell me. You…" She hesitated, but what the hell, they all knew about it anyway. "You kissed me, but you didn't tell me you were responsible for leaking the story."

"I never knew Gareth Roux was your father. Don only mentioned it during Zoe and Dale's wedding. I was going to talk to you about it this weekend—"

"And what? Lie to me? Give me a watered-down version of the facts?"

David stared at her, his hands resting on his hips. His eyes turned to slits. "I don't lie," he said in a clipped voice and turned to Caitlin.

"I heard Dana's car broke down, and I'm here to take her to Hermanus."

Caitlin glanced in her direction quickly. "I…" she began, but Rosa interrupted, pushing Dana toward the front door.

"What a splendid idea. I wasn't going to be able to keep Donato as long as I hoped; I have to go back to the restaurant. So now I can visit my grandbaby, and Caitlin doesn't have to drive all the way to Hermanus and drive back alone."

Dana ground her teeth. She was positive Rosa was embellishing the truth a little bit, and she was being coerced into going with David. She glared daggers at him, but he ignored her and kissed his mother.

She didn't want to spend any more time with him than was necessary, but she also would prefer Caitlin didn't drive all the way to Hermanus and back. And he knew it, damn it!

Swallowing her frustration, she said her goodbyes and followed David to his car.

AFTER AN HOUR, Dana still hadn't spoken a word, but David could feel every pulse of the resentment just about radiating from her body.

The only words she'd spoken were to direct him to her house.

"You are obviously angry with me, and I want to explain the whole thing to you, but I want to know you'll listen." He turned down another street she indicated.

"So talk." She crossed her arms and leaned back against the seat.

David turned his head and stared at her, not sure whether he wanted to throttle her or kiss her. "Why did you speak to Sean Murray?"

Her eyes flashed. "Because I've been looking for answers for two years, and he was the first definite lead I got. Talking to the police has been a fruitless exercise. I eventually started emailing newspapers and got hold of Sean. And he told me that you"—she pointed at him—"were the one who implicated my dad. And my dad"—she swallowed—"is innocent! I know him. He would never have stolen other people's money; he would never have committed suicide. And I have to prove it; nobody else is interested in clearing his name. That's why I'm trying to find out what happened. That's why I talked to Sean. I hoped I would get answers. What I didn't expect to hear was that a guy who kissed me is the same person who spilled the story. And didn't think to tell me about it."

Her accusations sliced through him like a sharp sword. Wow. He hadn't known she was looking into her father's case and that she was talking to other journalists about it. If he had, he would have made time to talk to her on the plane, but, of course, talking didn't seem important when he was around Dana lately.

It wasn't anything he hadn't told himself before. He should never have taken half the story to the editor, but he'd wanted to make sure he would get the front page when he had finished the story.

Well, he got the front page, just not on the day he'd wanted it and not with the facts all sorted out.

He nodded. "You're right about the fact that I was the one who took the story to the editor of the paper. But like I said, when I met you, when I kissed you…" He turned and looked at her. "I didn't know you were Gareth Roux's daughter—"

"This is my house." Dana pointed toward a small cottage.

David looked around as he stopped in front of Dana's house. They were in the older part of town, and this street was lined with old-charm cottages.

"And," he continued, "you don't have all the facts. For one, the story I took to the editor didn't mention your dad. Well, except in the margin, but I was still…" He interrupted himself. "Can we continue this inside?" he asked.

She shook her head adamantly. "No! I've done enough talking for the day." Her eyes welled up, and she got out of the car quickly.

BLINDED BY TEARS, Dana stumbled toward her front door, trying to find her key. Her only thought was to reach the sanctuary that was home.

"Dana!" David's voice bellowed from behind her, but she ignored him.

He came up behind her but she stubbornly refused to look at him. Tears were clogging up her throat; she wouldn't be able to talk anyway. A tear slipped down her cheek and, furiously, she wiped it away. But then another one followed and another.

Gentle fingers took her key and opened her front door.

David steered her inside and closed the door behind them. He pulled her close and rested his chin on her head. For minutes he stood like that, just holding her.

She tried to hang on to her anger, her hurt, but it was so wonderful not to be the strong one, not be the one doing the comforting but to be comforted.

When she was little, her dad was the one who'd pick her up and hug her when she cried. He was the caretaker, the caregiver. And ever since his death, the role had become hers. And she was just so tired of always trying to be the strong one.

But she had no choice; she had to get to the bottom of what had happened to her dad. And she definitely couldn't let David seduce her into believing his version of the truth.

She pushed against his shoulders, and he let her go.

"Will you please listen to what I have to say?" David

asked.

Dana hesitated. A headache was threatening to split her head in two. She was hurting so much. It was a struggle to keep the tears at bay.

She wanted to be angry with David, wanted to hate him, but if she was honest, deep down, she wanted there to be a different story. How did she deal with all these conflicting emotions?

Nodding, she walked toward the kitchen part of the open-plan living area. Fortunately, she'd cleaned her house yesterday. She grimaced. The main reason was that she knew David would be visiting over the weekend, and she'd been looking forward to seeing him again.

And now everything was such a mess. She should have listened to her instincts and stayed away from journalists.

She looked at her watch. Four o'clock.

Unfortunately, way too early for a glass of wine. Even though she'd rather crawl under her blankets, she would have to offer David something. He did drive her all the way to Hermanus.

"Would you like coffee or tea?" she asked David and rubbed her forehead.

He was coming closer and took a seat at the counter. "Coffee would be nice, thanks. Headache?"

She nodded and put the kettle on.

"Do you have something to take?"

She nodded and pointed toward a small cupboard. "I'll

get something later." She took out the coffee mugs.

David got up, opened the cupboard door, and took out the bottle of pain pills. He got a glass from the counter, poured water in it, and handed the pills and the glass to her.

Her throat clogged up.

"Thanks," she got out before swallowing down the pills.

"I love your house," David murmured as he looked around.

"Thanks, it's an old place, but I love the wooden floors, window panes," she said putting the mugs on the counter and looking around.

It was also home, her space. Her mother had tried to get her to sell it after her dad's death and move in with her, but this was the one thing she'd been trying desperately to hang on to. This was the one place she could find calm, where her life seemed ordinary, tranquil even.

"So tell me your version of the story." She didn't even try to hide her skepticism.

DAVID THREW A last glance at Dana's neat house.

Everything was done in white, and it was obvious she'd tried to create an uncluttered space in which there was order, where things were sorted and filed, a place where she could forget about the turmoil that was her life at the moment.

He put his mug down and looked at Dana.

Dark circles under her eyes gave her a haunted look. She

seemed lost somehow, and he had to clamp down his urge to take her into his arms.

He couldn't remember ever feeling this way about a woman. Dana was hurting, and he wanted to take care of her, wanted to make all the bad stuff go away. But the determined lift of her chin in spite of her obvious distress was a clear indication she was used to solving her own problems.

"As I've said, I was the one who took the story to the editor; that is true. And, yes, I wanted to make sure the front page would be mine, but I told him I still had to verify some facts," he began and continued to tell her what had happened.

She listened without interrupting him until he'd finished. At last, her stiff shoulders relaxed somewhat.

"Why did you write my dad's name in the margin?"

He hesitated. "He was one of the people my source said I should talk to. In the original article I wrote, I mentioned the fact that several independent financial advisors marketed Hastings's product as well. What I didn't do, and should have done before I took the story to the editor, was to talk to these guys, your dad included."

"So you didn't even know whether my dad was involved in any way?" she asked, stunned.

David rubbed his face. How much should he tell her?

"David, tell me what you know," Dana insisted.

"Okay. Fact. The financial advisors who were involved

were selling Hastings's product. Fact. They earned large commissions from Hastings for every deal. This is on record. What I don't know is whether your dad was selling the product and to what degree the financial advisors were privy to what was going on, whether they knew that Hastings was running a Ponzi scheme and wasn't investing their clients' money but spending it. I quit the job after the editor hijacked my story, joined my brothers, and made sure I ignored the story."

Dana chewed on her lower lip. "How culpable would my dad have been? That is to say, if he did in fact market this specific product at all."

"Look, as I've said, I never spoke to him, but if he did sell it, he was supposed to make sure every deal he offered a client was aboveboard, that the financial institution he was representing was legitimate. So, if he was involved, I'm afraid he would not have gotten off scot-free. I don't know what happened to the other advisors involved. I didn't follow the rest of the story, but I suspect that, at the very least, they would have had to pay back their clients' money and/or were given a jail sentence."

Devastated, Dana looked at David, a tear rolling down her cheek.

He jumped up and picked her up. Damn it, that was it! She struggled, but he ignored it and walked to the couch where he sat down, his arms still around her.

She turned her face into his neck and quietly cried. She

clutched his shirt, and her body shivered against his. A tenderness he didn't understand made him gather her closer while his hands moved rhythmically over her back.

He wished he could miraculously take her hurt away, but he also knew that wasn't possible.

Her phone rang. She lifted her head and took her phone from her bag then sighed and closed her eyes for a moment.

"I have to take this," she said and got up. "Hi, Mom," she said as she walked away and stood with her back turned toward him.

"I was in Cape Town … I'm sorry, I didn't know…"

It was quiet for a few minutes.

"But I gave you money last week." Dana lowered her voice but the frustration in her tone was unmistakable.

"My car broke down. I'm not sure—" Silence again.

"Okay, Mother, I'll see what I can do." She sighed resignedly as she hung up. She stood for a while before turning back to face him.

Chapter Seven

DANA WALKED BACK slowly to where David was still sitting on the couch. She wished she could simply walk past him, close her bedroom door, and pretend she never had a telephone conversation with her mother.

But he'd obviously heard the whole thing. "You probably heard that, right?" she asked.

He nodded.

"It's my mom. This whole thing with my dad hit her hard. She is struggling to cope with what happened. And, on top of everything, she is struggling financially."

"This has nothing to do with me, but didn't your dad provide for her?"

Dana nodded. "Yes, he did, but I suppose with every-thing getting so expensive..." She shrugged.

"Don't you have a brother?" David asked. "Does he help out?"

"He lives and works in Dubai. My mom visited him over Christmas last year, so he does his bit."

David stared at her for a moment. "Have you spoken to your mother's financial advisor? I assume your dad would have had someone look after his affairs."

Dana nodded. "Yes, but my mother and he sorted out my dad's things."

David leaned forward. "Look, I know this is none of my business, but I suggest you talk to this guy. Try to find out exactly what her situation is. Maybe, I don't know, it's just a matter of helping her manage her affairs?"

"More coffee?" Ignoring David's question, she picked up the mugs. The last thing she wanted was for David to become involved in her family problems. It was humiliating enough that he'd had to bring her home today.

Behind her, David moved and she felt his presence. He took the mugs from her and put them behind him on the kitchen counter. "No, thanks. What about your car?"

"I'll sort it out, thanks," she said, trying a smile. "I've been waiting for the school break before looking for a new car, so now I have time."

"I'm staying at Don's house for the weekend," David said. "If you like, I could pick you up…"

She lifted her chin. "I'm quite capable of buying my own car, thank you." She turned toward the front door. "Well, thank you for bringing me home… I'm sure you have other things to do…"

She trailed off. David had moved quickly and was standing in front of her.

"Oh, I have lots of other things to do…" He growled, his eyes flashing once before he bent his head down. Without closing his eyes, he caught her bottom lip between his teeth, much the same way she'd bitten him a few days ago.

A shiver ran down her spine; his eyes darkened.

"Dana," he whispered and pulled her closer, "you make me want things…" He swept his hands up her back, and he molded her body to his.

This could not be happening again! She'd had a horrible day. From what she'd discovered, it sounded as if David had been directly responsible for what had happened to her dad, her car had broken down, her mother was driving her crazy, but when David touched her, kissed her, her body simply took over the workings of her brain and all of her worries seemed to fade.

His scent filled her nostrils, pulled her in until she was only aware of sensations. Special. Safe.

Treasured. Adored. That was how he made her feel.

But it wasn't real. He lived in a world light years re-moved from hers. She pushed against him, and he lifted his head.

"I'm fine. Thanks for all your help, but I'm—"

"Fine," David said sardonically. "I can see exactly how fine you are."

"Good." She stiffened her spine. She opened the front door. "Goodbye."

David held her gaze a moment longer. He brushed the back of his hand against her cheek.

"Good night," he said and left.

She locked the door behind him, switched off the lights, and walked to her room. A big hole opened up inside of her, and a tear escaped and rolled over her face. Angrily, she wiped it away and sniffled.

Crying never did anyone any good. Tomorrow she would try to find out how involved her dad had been in Hastings's dealings. But for now, she was going to take a long bath and try not to think.

FULL OF ENERGY, David knocked on Dana's front door. He couldn't wait to tell her what he'd discovered. He'd hardly slept last night. He knocked again. It was quiet inside. He pressed his ear against the door. Finally, he could hear movement in the background.

It wasn't that early; surely she was up by now? For the first time since he'd taken a shower, he looked at his watch and groaned out loud. It was only seven o'clock.

The door flew open, and he lost every single rational thought. Dana was standing there in a pair of pink pajamas—if that was what he could call the tiny strappy top and pair of sexy shorts she was wearing. Her hair was mussed, and it was clear she'd just gotten out of bed.

Blood pooled below his middle, and for a moment he felt quite light-headed. He steadied himself by clutching the door frame on either side of him.

"David!" she grumbled and rubbed her eyes. "What the

hell? Do you know what time it is?"

His blood was roaring so loudly in his ears, he barely made out what she was saying.

"It's a beautiful day." He tried one of his best smiles. "But, sorry, no, I didn't know it was this early. I haven't really slept," he tried to explain, as if his ramblings made complete sense.

She opened the door wider and rubbed her face. "Coffee." She groaned and turned her back on him. "I must have coffee."

He stumbled. Wow. What a sight. Her legs kind of went on and on and on. And the seriously tiny pair of shorts she was wearing lovingly cupped her tight bottom. Oh, man.

Taking deep breaths, he finally felt balanced enough to follow her. Ever since he'd kissed this woman, he'd been a bit off-kilter. His mouth lifted on one side. An interesting notion and one he wasn't sure what to make of.

DANA STRETCHED TO get the coffee from the top shelf, and David groaned behind her.

Frowning, she turned around to find David's eyes way below her middle. She looked down. Oh, bloody hell, she was still in her pajamas!

Now, wide awake, she inhaled audibly, and David lifted his gaze to meet hers.

"I'll…" She swallowed. His eyes were a dark, dark

brown, his nostrils flaring. "Get dressed." She moved sideways in the direction of her room.

He leaned against the counter, his gaze raking her from head to toe. Heat uncurled inside of her, and she forgot to breathe.

"Good idea." His voice was deliciously raspy.

She fled to her room.

Quickly, trying not to think about the heat she'd seen in David's eyes, she slipped into a pair of white jeans and a T-shirt. In the bathroom, she stared at her face. Her eyes sparkled; her cheeks were red. Groaning, she washed her face and tried to put makeup on with unsteady fingers. He had her heart racing, her blood heating, and she hadn't even had her first cup of coffee yet!

She found him pouring coffee into yesterday's mugs. He had to have washed them, as she hadn't bothered last night.

"Sit on that side of the counter." He motioned with his hand without looking at her. "Maybe if you're across from me, I'll be able to concentrate and remember what I have to tell you." Only then did he look up. His hands stilled; his eyes darkened.

Swearing softly, he put the coffee down and reached her in two strides. He cupped her face, rubbed his thumbs over her lower lip.

"I have to kiss you again," he murmured, before he bent down and caught her lips with his.

Dana put her hands on his shoulders to push him away,

but the minute his mouth settled over hers, she couldn't remember why she'd wanted to do that. Kissing David was becoming a habit. Her body was ready for the surge of pleasure that zipped through her, heating her blood and leaving her breathless.

He lifted his head slowly and kissed her forehead before he dropped his arms and turned away. Picking up his mug, he looked at her over his shoulder.

"You're like a fix I constantly need." He growled.

"Don't say things like that!" she said, blushing.

"It's the truth," he insisted and sat down, facing her. "But, although I would like nothing better than to cart you off to the nearest bed and make love to you until neither of us can see straight, I'm actually here because I found out something I think you would like to hear."

The first part of his sentence robbed her of her last breath, and it took a while before she was able to register what the second part of his sentence implied. "What did you hear?" She really hoped talking about something else would calm her hormones.

"Well, it turns out two of the other financial advisors whose names were mentioned two years ago are living near Hermanus. One lives in Caledon and one in Kleinmond. I thought we should try to get hold of them and see if we can talk to them, find out what they know."

Dana stared at David while his words sank in. "I've been focused on trying to find out what the police know, and I've only recently decided to contact the newspapers. I never even thought of getting in touch with the other financial advisors involved."

"Didn't Sean say anything about them?"

Dana grimaced and lowered her eyes. "I… didn't really give him a chance to say anything else other than…" She hesitated.

"I was the bad guy?" David asked.

She nodded. "Look, David, thanks for doing this, but it's not your problem. I've had time to think, and I accept your version of what happened. So you don't have any reason to get involved with my mess."

He put his mug down slowly, his lips moving into a smile. "Oh, I don't know. I like being where you are," he said, as if it was the most logical thing in the world. "So get your bag or whatever you'll need. I'll phone and see whether I can get hold of them. I briefly spoke to both of them two years ago, so hopefully they'll remember me."

"And that's a good thing? Most people aren't fond of journalists."

He shrugged. "I think they'll talk to us."

She hesitated. "You don't have to come with me. I can do this—"

"By yourself. I know," David interrupted. "I know you're brave. I know you're an independent woman who can do everything you want to on your own, but I'm here. I want to be close to you, and I can help. Also, I know I'm not responsible for what happened, but I should have made sure of my facts before I showed the story to the editor. And that was my mistake. One I'm trying to rectify now. Let me?" And the devastating Cavallo smile nearly had her falling off her chair.

Dana frowned and crossed her arms. "You're not playing fair," she mumbled.

"Oh, are we playing now?" he teased, and grabbing her hand, he pulled her up.

He pulled her closer and lost his smile. For a moment their bodies touched and she became aware of his desire. Light-headed, she shook her head and pulled away.

"M-my... um... my b-bag..." she stuttered and fled.

"Take your time," he called out. "I'll make some calls."

DAVID STARED AT Dana's retreating back. Only when she'd closed her bedroom door behind her could he exhale. Damn, the woman was killing him. Ever since he'd kissed her for the first time, he'd been walking around like a randy teenager.

Focus, Cavallo, focus. He scrolled down on his phone where he'd made a note of the names and telephone numbers of the men he was hoping they could see today. There was another number he wanted to phone first. This would be their first stop.

Chapter Eight

"WHERE ARE WE going now?" Dana asked when David took a turn to the left. "The N2 is that way." She pointed ahead of them.

"We're making a quick stop—I want to show you something."

She frowned but didn't say anything. The place was only two streets down, and a few minutes later he stopped in front of a big showroom full of cars.

Dana looked at him. "Why are we stopping here?" she asked, ice lacing her voice.

He got out of the car. "To look. We have time. You need a car; they sell cars."

"These are brand-new cars. I can't afford any of them," Dana said and stared straight ahead.

David walked around the car and opened her door. This had seemed such an obvious solution that he didn't understand why she was so stubborn.

"You can't know that if you don't look. Besides, they also have secondhand cars. Just look. You don't have to buy anything."

She sat, obviously fuming, for a few minutes more before she got reluctantly out of the car.

Clutching her bag under her arm, she turned to him. "I told you I can take care of myself, I can buy my own car, I can—"

He bent down and kissed her. It was the only way he could think of to shut her up. He lifted his head slightly and smiled down at her.

"I know. But here we are. Let's see what they have that might suit you."

She inhaled sharply and put one hand on her hip, but before she could say another word, he kissed her again. It seemed to get her to be quiet at least for one minute.

"You can't keep doing that." She hissed. "I'm—"

Before she could utter another word, he simply kissed her again. But this time, she bit his bottom lip again, as she had done not so long ago when he'd kissed her for the first time. And, like that time, his body reacted instantly. Blood pooled below his belt, leaving him breathless.

With a triumphant glint in her eyes, she turned way and walked toward the showroom. The little minx; she knew exactly what she did to him.

Groaning, he stood still, willing his body to return to normal. With a mocking glance over her shoulder, Dana entered the showroom, making it clear she knew exactly why he wasn't already following her.

He smiled and slowly followed her. She knew what she

did to him and blatantly used it. But two could play this game. There was no way he could leave her with the upper hand.

When he entered the big showroom, she was already talking to one of the salesmen. One who was standing way too close to her for his liking. He quickly joined them and slung an arm around her shoulders, staking his claim.

With a nod, the salesman smiled in his direction, indicating he'd received the message.

While Dana explained what she was looking for, David looked around and played with her hair with his fingers. She tried to move away, but he moved so he was behind her and put both his arms around her body.

"Well, sweetheart," he said, pulling her close to him, "I'm sure you'll find something here."

Dana turned her head and smiled up at him.

He didn't trust the light in her eyes, and a second later he knew why. She touched his face, and when he lifted his arms to pull her even closer, she slipped under his arm and skittered away to the secondhand car section.

"What can you tell me about this one?" she asked the salesman, smiling up at the guy.

DANA WAS BEGINNING to enjoy the whole thing.

David was obviously used to having his own way most of the time. But she could manage her own life and didn't need a rich man to help her out. He was probably trying to ease his conscience this way, but it wasn't necessary—she was fair enough to understand he wasn't the one responsible for what had happened to her dad.

But it was a heady feeling to see David Cavallo at a loss for words for once, to see that only a touch of her hand could rattle him. Although her own flirting was playing havoc with her hormones, if she was honest, she liked the way his eyes darkened as they had just now when she'd touched his face.

While batting her eyelashes at the salesman, she cast a furtive look in David's direction. His eyes narrowed, and it was clear he didn't like her flirting with another man. Which, of course, was all the motivation she needed to move a little bit closer to the poor guy.

The salesman talked and explained, opened doors, showed her the engine—all of which went way over her head. But she nodded, trying to look interested, although she'd known from the beginning she wouldn't be able to afford any of these cars.

"Well, thank you very much. I'm afraid I've wasted your time, but—"

"The price on this one?" David asked, coming closer.

Irritated, Dana turned to walk away, but when she heard the figure the salesman mentioned, she looked around, stunned.

"Really? I thought they'd go for a lot more."

"Well, normally they do." The salesman gave David a nervous look. "But we have a special today."

David started asking questions, and Dana walked around the car again while her brain was working overtime. She had enough saved to pay for the car, but now her mother wanted money again.

Her mother used to be a kindergarten teacher, and after her dad's death, Dana thought her mom would like to go back to teaching again. Dana had actually been able to find her a teaching job at the local primary school, but her mother had been horrified. How could Dana even think such a thing; she didn't have the stamina, etcetera, etcetera.

Maybe she should try to talk to her mother again. If she was prepared to work again, it would be such a big help. But maybe she was being selfish, maybe her mother was too frail.

"So, what do you think?" David's voice pulled her back.

"I... don't know. Let me think about it?" she said to the salesman.

"Of course, but we can talk about the price again. I could even go lower." He mentioned a figure.

Dana's eyes nearly popped out of her head. "Really? That sounds even better. I'll think—"

"What's to think about?" David interrupted. "This is a good make, you like it, it's available. What's more, you need a car."

Dana lifted her chin. "I said I'll think about it," she said before turning to the salesman again. "Thank you for your time. If you give me your card, I'll let you know."

"Of course." He handed her his card.

On their way back to the car, David flung his arms around her shoulders again. "You're going to take the car. You could just as well have signed the papers."

Dana looked up at him. "I said I'll think about it. There are a lot of things I have to consider."

David opened the car door for her, and she slid in. "I know. But you've made another conquest back there. If you decide to take it, the salesman will probably offer to deliver the car to you."

Dana nodded. She hadn't even thought about the fact that come Monday, David would probably be back in Cape Town. Restlessly, she moved in her seat while he walked around to his side. She'd miss him. And she didn't know that she liked the feeling.

Within the span of a few days David Cavallo had become an integral part of her life. She was even buying a car with him!

"SO, WHO IS this guy?" Dana asked as they stopped in front of a huge house in the beautiful small coastal village of Kleinmond.

"Sam Jordan." David opened his door. "He was one of the financial advisors I spoke to two years ago."

Dana stared at the big house. It was a huge place sprawling over what looked like at least three plots and had a lovely view of the sea. She didn't know much about real estate, but she knew a house with this kind of view would be pricey. Very pricey.

What had happened had clearly not affected this Sam guy. If he had been punished in any way, he'd bounced back quickly enough.

David opened her car door.

Frowning, she got out. "You don't have to open car doors for me, David. I can do it—"

Before she could finish the sentence, his mouth was descending on hers.

She tried to keep his mouth from reaching her by pushing against his shoulders. "Don't do that..." She moaned into his mouth.

Then her brain cells ceased to function.

When he lifted his head, they were both breathing hard. "If you keep telling me you can do things yourself, we'll end up making love before the end of the day." David growled and closed the car door. He took her hand and, stunned, she let him.

Making love. Immediately, the two words conjured images of their entwined bodies. The heat from his hand around hers spread lightning-quick through her bloodstream, making it difficult to breathe.

"David, d-don't," she stuttered.

He pulled her hand through his arm and walked in the

direction of the front door. "Then accept that I want to help you." He smiled, and lifting her hand, he kissed her fingers. "Let's find out what really happened, and then we can get on with the rest of our lives."

That warm feeling she kept experiencing when he was around opened up inside of her again, and she swallowed. If she wasn't careful, this man might steal her heart. Having had her fair share of bad dates, some of which her friend Caitlin had blogged about, she'd learned that most men are only interested in their own comfort and are usually so full of themselves they hardly noticed anyone else who needed help.

But not David. It was as if he knew what she needed even before she realized it herself. But she had to remember this was a temporary thing. As he'd just said, after this, they'd be able to go on with their lives.

He was on a mission to help her, but once the puzzle had been solved, once he'd done what he'd set out to do, she'd probably only see him again at family gatherings. As a family friend. Which was a good thing. Wasn't it?

They'd reached the front door and David knocked.

HALF AN HOUR later David drove them away from the big house. Dana was silent. He glanced at her. He was learning to read her body language.

When she became quiet, like she was at the moment, she was trying to sort things out in her head.

"He was very friendly," David said.

She turned her head in his direction. "Very."

"But…" they said simultaneously.

Dana smiled. "Yeah, but… His smile never wavered, but he was a bit vague, don't you think? He never answered a direct question."

David nodded. "I agree. For one, he never answered your question about whether he knew for sure if your dad was also selling Hastings's product. I wonder why."

"Plus, I still don't know what his part in the whole thing was. He managed to evade all questions about that."

"Well, he definitely marketed the product and received commissions. But it's obvious he's never spent any time in jail. The guy we're going to see in Caledon, Toby Johnson, went to jail for a year. There were several articles about him, but I couldn't find anything else on Sam. And he evaded all our questions about that."

Dana fell silent for a few minutes. "He has a big house," she remarked.

"It would be easy enough to find out when he bought it and what the price was," David said.

"You could do that?"

David smiled. "Finding things out was my job for about ten years, remember. I was an investigative reporter; I investigated."

Dana became quiet again, and David turned onto the N2 toward Caledon. This part of the Western Cape was known as the Overberg, literally meaning over the mountain. In front of them lay the beautiful countryside. Nowadays kilometers of vineyards could be found alongside the highway, but the region was mostly known for producing wheat.

It was a beautiful summer day, and although talking to these people was not something he wanted to be doing, driving through this part of the country with Dana next to him was quite something.

"So, why didn't you finish your story two years ago? I mean, I know you were angry with the editor, but didn't you want to know how the whole thing ended? That is, if you don't mind my asking?"

"No, it's fine. It's not as if I haven't asked myself the same question, you know? But I was so ticked off, had been for a while actually, and this story was just the final straw. It was also around that time Don asked us if we wanted to join his business. For me it was a no-brainer. Although I loved the reporting bit, the politics wasn't for me. The paper I was working for was also moving in a direction I wasn't comfortable with. Yes, I believe the public has a right to know, but it was relying more and more on a sensational kind of reporting, wanting us to draw conclusions, and as far as I'm concerned that wasn't my job. My job was to report facts. That's why I was so angry. I very specifically told the editor I was still checking facts, but he wanted to sell newspapers and ran with the story. So I simply walked away, turning my back on everything."

"So, why do you want to get involved again?"

He glanced at her. She was genuinely puzzled.

"Surely you must know why?" He smiled, but she gave him a blank look. "Because of you," he said simply. "You seem so confident that your dad could not have been involved. And to tell you the truth, I've never stopped thinking about the case. Your dad's death has been haunting me ever since I found out."

She folded her hands and looked down. "The dad I knew was a caring, loving man. He wouldn't knowingly have been dishonest—it was simply not part of his nature."

"You were close?"

Dana nodded. "Very. He was my rock, my go-to person. If it hadn't been for Caitlin and her mom, I don't know how I would have coped after his death."

"You and your mother don't get along?" David asked then held his breath. Would she answer such a question?

She shrugged. "We're just so different, and she struggles to cope with life." She didn't elaborate, but sadness filled her voice.

He couldn't imagine another kind of mother than his own. Even though she had always worked as a chef, first for other people and then in her own restaurant, her children had always been, and still were, her priority in life. And as far as he was concerned, that was how mothers were supposed to operate—they handled things, they hugged, and they wiped tears. But it sounded like in Dana's case she was the one having to do the hugging and the handling.

Taking her hand in his, they drove the last few kilometers in silence.

Chapter Nine

"WELL, CLEARLY THIS guy hasn't been able to get back on his feet," Dana mumbled under her breath as David knocked on the front door of Toby Johnson's house.

The small house was in obvious need of paint. The door opened a fraction, and a tired-looking older woman looked suspiciously around the door.

"I don't want to buy anything," she said crossly and started to close the door.

"We're here to see Mr. Johnson." David gave her one of his winning smiles.

The door stopped. Irritated, Dana rolled her eyes. It would appear, no matter what her age, no woman was immune to that killer smile.

"I phoned him earlier this morning, and he said he'd be home." David smiled again, and this time the woman opened the door widely.

She nodded and showed them in. "Yes, sorry. He mentioned it. He's in the sitting room, over there." She pointed to a door across the entrance.

The house was dark and musty-smelling.

Uncomfortable, Dana glanced around. Here was no display of worldly goods as in the Jordan household. It looked as if they were struggling to make ends meet, but the dining-room table looked new.

A man was sitting close to the window in the small room, staring outside, coughing every now and then.

"These people have come to talk to you, Toby," his wife said.

He turned his head toward them, still coughing. "Yes, you're the journalist who talked to me two years ago, the one who phoned earlier this morning?" He shook David's hand.

"Yes, thank you for seeing us," David said. "This is Dana Roux."

Dana stepped forward, and the man inhaled audibly. "Gareth Roux's daughter?" he asked, clearly shaken.

"Yes, I am." Dana sat down on a chair near him. She didn't know what was wrong with him, but he sounded ill.

Still coughing, he smiled tiredly. "Have asthma, jail didn't help, the medicine's expensive." He wheezed.

"We don't want to take up too much of your time, Mr. Johnson, but I'm trying to find out to what degree my dad was involved in the Hastings's scheme." Dana said directly. This was no time for beating around the bush.

Another fit of coughing racked his body but he kept shaking his head. His wife handed him a glass of water, and he finally settled down.

"But your dad wasn't involved. I never understood why he was taken into custody. We spoke two years ago, just before the story hit the newspapers. He heard about Hastings's scheme from one of his clients and contacted me to find out whether I knew anything about it. He didn't trust the high interest rates clients of the scheme spoke about and didn't think it could be sustainable. Of course, I confirmed the high interest rate. What I didn't know was that things were already going downhill—the article in the newspaper was the last straw. Investors stopped, there wasn't any new money coming in, and the well dried up overnight.

"I was happy enough to earn the big commission and didn't ask too many questions while it went well, stupid idiot that I was. Typical of these types of schemes, the initial payouts were enormous and investors were happy. But when no new clients brought in more money, we all realized what was going on. Hastings never invested the money in new buildings as the clients were promised, instead he used it to support his own lavish lifestyle. That is of course exactly the kind of thing that brings down a Ponzi scheme."

Frowning, Dana stared at the man. So many thoughts were racing through her head, it was difficult to grasp everything Toby was saying. "So what was my dad's reaction?"

"Well, he was going to contact the financial services board about Hastings's scheme. He was worried for his clients. I told Sam Jordan about your father's concerns—

don't know whether you know him?"

Dana nodded, and Toby continued between fits of coughing.

"Sam thought your dad was overreacting. But next thing I knew, the story was in the newspaper, your dad was taken into custody, and was found dead. I got hauled in and eventually had to go to jail."

Dumbfounded, Dana sat back in her chair trying to make sense of what she'd just heard.

"So you're saying Dana's dad would not have been involved in the scheme, because he didn't trust what was going on?" David asked.

Toby nodded. "But his name was mentioned in the initial newspaper report. He was taken in for questioning. Why he ended up in the police cells, I don't know. As far as I know, there wasn't anything that could have linked him to the whole mess. But he was dead before he even called his lawyer."

"I know, and I thought that was so strange. He and his lawyer were also friends. I never understood why my dad didn't call him," Dana said.

Toby's frail body doubled over in a coughing fit. Eventually, he regained his breath. "Maybe he was silenced; I don't know."

"What do you mean?" Dana's heart hammered anxiously.

Toby leaned back against the chair and closed his eyes. "I

don't trust any of these bastards. But I've already said too much." He opened one eye. "You may find that not everyone likes you poking into old affairs," he said and closed his eye again.

"One more thing, why did you go to jail and not Sam Jordan?" asked David.

He shrugged. "Apparently there was no paper trail linking him to any transaction."

"But how is that possible? He must have earned commissions for his dealings?" Dana asked.

"There was talk of money laundering…" Toby got out before he coughed again.

"Money laundering?" Surprised, Dana frowned. She couldn't remember anyone mentioning this before.

Toby nodded and leaned back against the chair. "Abalone poachers," he wheezed. "It's a huge money-making business in Gansbaai, the little village on the other side of Hermanus. According to rumors, Hastings and these scumbags were in cahoots. It was a win-win situation; at least that's what they thought. Hastings made money; they laundered their dirty money."

David nodded his head slowly. "I've heard the rumors but never got around to following up on that. So what you're saying is that Jordan's commissions never went through any bank, so he couldn't be linked to any transaction?"

But another fit of coughing overtook the frail body, and his wife motioned for them to leave.

OUTSIDE, DANA BREATHED in the fresh air. David took her hand in his.

"You okay?" he asked.

"I don't know." Dana looked back over her shoulder. "He's been in jail and has obviously lost whatever money he made during the scheme. From all accounts, Sam Jordan was involved but there is no money trail. So he never went to jail and lives in a mansion overlooking the sea?"

David's mind was racing and adrenaline was pumping through his system. "There is a story here; I can smell it." He helped her into the car.

"What are you thinking?" Dana asked as they drove away.

David was silent for a few minutes. "I don't know, but something doesn't feel right."

"What do you mean?"

"Well, the man sounds quite ill, but is it real or was he putting on an act?"

Surprised, Dana looked at him. "You really think so? But he gave us so much information about the money laundering scheme and…"

"Yeah, a lot of information, something I also find strange." He tried to figure out why he wasn't convinced by the man's story.

"So, what do we do now? What do you think?" Dana asked.

He turned to look at her. She was clearly worried—a frown marred her forehead; her hands were clutched together tightly.

He touched her hands and smiled. "I think I have a beautiful woman with me and that it's time for lunch." He smiled, trying to lighten the mood. He looked at her before he turned onto the highway. "And I know just the place."

"You know what I mean. What do you think about what Toby said? About the money laundering, about my dad being silenced? Do you think he made it up? Is it all linked?"

David took her hand. "I don't know what to think. But I still have my contacts and will ask around. We can see what else is available from old online newspaper articles, but that we can do tonight. Let's have lunch. I think much better on a full stomach."

"You don't have to buy me lunch," she said crossly.

"I know," he agreed. "But I want to. There is this excellent restaurant in the Hemel and Aarde Valley. The food is divine—even my mother likes it. I also like their wine."

He held his breath. He wanted her to forget about all the bad stuff for at least a few hours, but would she be able to relax?

She sighed and stared out the window. "Heaven and earth—such a beautiful name for the valley despite its sad history. Did you know they kept lepers in this valley two centuries ago?"

"I read about that when I was doing a story on the original landowner who, incidentally, also had leprosy."

"I didn't know that," she said with interest and he began telling her everything he knew on the topic. It wasn't a very happy topic but would get her mind off all the bad things she was worrying about, even if only for a few hours.

By the time they took the turnoff into the valley, he could feel her relaxing for the first time since that morning. It pleased him enormously to know, despite everything that was going on in her life, she could unwind around him.

As they drove on, she pointed toward the various wine farms along the way, and they discussed wine. He was happy, he realized after a while. And although he was mostly happy with life, this feeling was something more. But what? Contentment? No, not quite. Completion?

Wow—that was an unexpected word. But then, what he was feeling around this woman was unexpected.

They reached the turnoff for the restaurant and turned onto the road. He glanced in Dana's direction. She was looking at him.

He stopped the car, leaned over, and kissed her.

"Wh—" she began when he lifted his head.

"Just because." He smiled, put the car back in gear, and drove up to the parking bay.

IT WAS A beautiful day. Dana's shoulders relaxed, and she smiled at David as they walked toward the restaurant.

He opened the door for her and took her elbow. While he was talking to reception, she moved closer to the big windows overlooking the valley.

From here, she could even get a glimpse of the sea.

"Come on," he said behind her and took her hand. "We have a table by the window. You can enjoy the view all through lunch."

When they were seated, he looked at the wine list. "What kind of wine would you like?"

They decided on a white pinot grigio and looked over the menu. While David was placing their order, she had to force herself to look away from him. His smile. The poor waitress was just about falling over her feet.

When the waitress left, David took her hand. "So, you're a teacher. Tell me about your class."

"Surely you're not interested in—"

"I'm interested in everything you do," he said without taking his eyes off of her.

IT WAS EARLY evening when they stopped in front of her little house. Surprised, Dana looked up. She and David had been talking nonstop since they left the restaurant, so she hadn't even realized they were back in Hermanus.

The last few hours had been surreal. David had joked and talked and made sure she never had a moment to even think about her problems.

David was skilled at making conversation, and she found herself telling him things that she'd only shared with Caitlin up to now. And he actually listened—not something most men do.

And then there was his smile. Oh, my! She'd never before experienced the full impact of his smile but it was devastating, to say the least. She literally had to force herself to look away from him otherwise she might have started drooling. The man was way too handsome for her tender heart.

"Thank you…" she started to say and turned to David, but he was already out of the car and opening the trunk.

Before she could move, he was at her door, opening it. "You're not getting rid of me that quickly." He helped her out.

"I thought you might want to get back to Cape Town." She noticed his laptop in his hand.

"I'm here until tomorrow." He lifted his laptop. "Let's see what else we can dig up about Hastings and Sam Jordan."

"David…" she began, but he put the fingers of one hand over her lips.

"We've talked about this." He took her hand as they walked toward the front door. "This whole thing has bugged me long enough. I want to find out what the real story is."

Dana opened the front door and walked into her house, trying to decide what she was feeling.

Relaxed. That was it. She was so relaxed she didn't have the energy to be irritated with David for wanting to help.

She inhaled sharply. It was so strange—to be able to share her worry with someone, to be able to voice her concerns about what she should do next. Caitlin had been the only person she ever opened up to, but ever since her friend had gotten married, Dana hadn't wanted to bother Caitlin with her problems, and she'd been bottling up so many feelings.

She turned to David. "Thanks for today, especially the lunch. I needed that." Smiling, she rolled her shoulders. "I think my shoulders are kink-free for the first time in... I don't know how long." She started toward the kitchen. "Would you like something to drink?"

But David grabbed her hand and put his laptop down. "Turn around so that I can make sure." He pushed at her shoulders.

"Make sure of what?"

"Whether you are kink-free, as you put it." He smiled, and she let him turn her so her back was against his body.

Warm hands folded over her shoulders and started kneading her muscles.

A groan inadvertently escaped when his fingers dug into her muscles.

"Mmmm," he whispered against her ear, "not completely relaxed, it would seem."

His words sent shivers down her spine, but she wasn't

feeling cold at all. A lethargic feeling stole over her, and she let her head fall back against David's shoulder. He pulled her body close to his, sliding his hands up and down her arms.

The movement was gentle, meant to soothe, but her body had other ideas and moved restlessly. As if he was reading her mind, his hands moved to her sides, slowly moving up and down, up and down. His fingers grazed her breasts, and her breath hitched far back in her throat.

"What?" David whispered in her ear, but she couldn't talk. "Is this what you want?" he asked and cupped her breasts.

Still unable to speak, she moved her hands behind her and clutched his legs. She couldn't form a coherent word even if her life depended on it.

Sensation after sensation crashed over her; sensory impulses were sending her nerve endings into overdrive until the roaring in her ears blocked out everything else. The only thing that mattered was stilling this insane craving inside her. And the only person who could do that was David.

He spun her around, and with one movement he lifted her. Her legs found their way around his body, her arms around his neck.

"You sure about this?" he asked hoarsely.

Still unable to speak, she lifted her top over her head. His eyes darkened, and with an oath, he hitched her higher.

"Hang on—which way is your room?" His breath was labored.

She pointed behind her, her eyes never leaving his.

"You're killing me, you know that?" He growled and swooped down for a kiss.

Chapter Ten

THE MINUTE HIS mouth found hers, she knew she wanted this man with a need that was staggering. The bedroom was too far away. Desperately, her fingers found the buttons on his shirt, and she pulled and tugged, her only thought that she wanted to touch him, wanted to find out whether her dreams did justice to reality.

With an oath, he lifted his head and dragged his shirt over his head, his eyes molten chocolate.

"Last chance," he warned, his eyes glittering.

But his voice was far away. Her eyes had zoomed in on his six-pack, and her hands slid adoringly over the hard contours before her sluggish brain cells could work. Her fingers stroked and caressed every muscle until his skin quivered beneath her touch. His heart tripped under her hand, and she lifted her gaze to his.

His eyes were half closed, his nostrils flaring, the proof of his desire throbbing against her stomach, and she was lost. She snaked her arms around his neck, and brought his head down and had just one thought—she wanted to become part of this man so badly, it was burning her up.

SOMEWHERE A VOICE was calling out, telling him to take it slowly, but his body was functioning on instinct, ignoring any rational reasoning. Because with Dana in his arms, the logical workings of his brain simply ceased to function.

Her upper body was firmly pressed against his. His fingers sought and found the clasp behind her back. Finally, he could unhook the sexy pink satin and lace number and remove it. His hands found her lushness, and his knees buckled.

"The bed…" He breathed in between kisses.

"Too far away," Dana whispered and smiled.

He had a moment to gape at her before his heated blood rushed through his body, making it impossible to speak.

His head bent down and he slipped his tongue around a rock-hard nipple She cried out his name. The sound echoed through him, egging him on, heating his blood.

Her hands fumbled with his belt, and swearing with frustration, he dragged his mouth away from her. He put her down and without taking his eyes off of her, got rid of his jeans. She lowered her eyes, watching his every movement.

When her eyes widened, he barked out a laugh.

"Like what you see?" he teased, and pulled down the zipper on her jeans.

Her eyes were nearly black with desire. He dropped down, yanking her jeans all the way down. All she was left wearing was a tiny scrap of pink satin. He had difficulty breathing, difficulty remembering who the hell he was.

With lust raging through him, it was impossible to give a name to the other feelings that were hurtling through him. But he wanted, he craved, he desired, he needed. Her. Just her.

He closed his hands around her ankles, moved up over silken skin, reveled in softness, felt heat under his fingertips until they reached the place his whole being was focused on.

Her scent lured him closer while he got rid of the last piece of clothing. His hands slid up. She was wet and ready for him.

DANA HAD LOST all ability to speak a while ago.

Sensation after sensation racked her body. When David's fingers found her, her legs gave way beneath her, and she fell forward into his arms.

"I wasn't finished." He smiled, and his fingers went right back to where they were.

Her breath hitched in her throat, and she pulled his head down. His kiss was wet, greedy, demanding. And she gave willingly, passionately, putting everything he was making her feel into the kiss.

A vortex picked her up and swept her along. She kept spinning and spinning, moving closer and closer to an edge she'd never been on before until, finally, she let go and went over the abyss—falling and falling and falling.

IN AWE, DAVID looked down at her. Her eyes opened, still glazed with desire.

"I've never seen anything so beautiful," he whispered and raised himself over her.

Her hands landed on his arms. "I want to touch you," she whispered, moving her hands downward.

But he shook his head. "I can't wait." With one movement, he pushed into her.

He tried to keep his eyes on her, tried to make this last, he'd waited a lifetime for this moment. But with her heat surrounding him, her eyes darkening, he was unable to do anything else but pull her closer and lose himself in her.

They began spinning away. He held on tightly, not wanting to let go, ever. Passion blinded him, and his other senses took over. The soft, luxurious, velvety texture of her skin nearly drove him insane. Her intoxicating scent surrounded him, and her unique taste filled a hunger he'd been unaware of until now.

DANA'S EYES FLEW open. For a few seconds she hovered in that empty space between dreams and reality before everything came crashing in.

Life would never be the same. Ever. She wasn't certain of anything else—but that she knew. She turned her head but even before she did, she could feel it—David wasn't next to her.

They'd finally made it to the bed. She put her arms over her eyes. Images of what had happened during the night kept popping up. David's muscled body above hers, his magical hands discovering, caressing every centimeter of her body, their legs entwined, and his eyes—dark with desire, lazy in the aftermath of lovemaking, heating up when he kissed her, laughing at her when she blushed.

This was temporary; she knew that. She was a teacher at a local high school; he was a billionaire and a co-owner of a string of hotels. She seldom left the small town where she made her living; he flew all over the world. And she was probably one of many women he'd spent a night with.

But for her it had been a once-in-a-lifetime experience, and what had happened between her and David was something she'd carry in her heart forever.

There was a footstep outside her door. She smelled coffee.

The door to the bedroom opened, and David walked in with two mugs on a tray, wearing only his jeans.

"Good morning, beautiful," he sang, putting the tray on the stand and sitting down next to her.

Dana tried to swallow, tried to speak, but her mouth was dry, her body started humming, and she could only look helplessly at him.

David stilled, his eyes darkened, and he shot his hands out to haul her against him.

Pushing his fingers into her hair, he devoured her mouth.

"Damn, I thought last night would have eased the want, but it's worse. This constant need to have you is worse," he scolded and claimed her mouth again.

This was not supposed to happen again. The night was over; life had to continue. That was her last rational thought. David kicked off his jeans, and she held out her arms. This was what she wanted. It was that simple.

DAVID STARED AT the computer, frowning. He was trying to concentrate, trying to make sense of what he was reading. But it was difficult. He kept looking in the direction of Dana's bedroom door, waiting for her to appear.

It was nearly time for lunch, and he'd finally realized that if he wanted to see what he could find out from old newspapers, he'd have to get out of Dana's room so she could get dressed. Again.

They tried showering together, dressing together, but each time they'd ended up in bed. Just a glimpse of her long legs, of her ample breasts, and he was like a hormone-driven teenager. He had absolutely no self-control around this woman.

And he wasn't sure he liked it.

He felt her before he saw her. He turned his head and there she was, walking toward him. Something shifted inside him.

"Come here." He held out his hand.

"David…" she began but took his hand.

"I have to touch you," he insisted and pulled her onto his lap.

With his fingers, he lightly traced the outline of her face. "You're beautiful."

She shuddered.

And then he had to kiss her again. And just like that, the fire was back in his blood, the need to make her his again raging inside him.

"WHAT ARE YOU doing?" David asked from behind her.

It was lunchtime. They'd showered again.

She'd fled the bedroom before she could attack him one more time. My goodness, she had absolutely no willpower when it came to David Cavallo. One look from his heated eyes, and she turned into a wanton hussy.

She was not going to turn around.

"I'm making omelets," she said, trying to sound cheerful instead of lustful. "Get us the plates, will you?" She still didn't look in his direction.

"It's not going to work, you know." He folded his arms around her from behind.

She groaned. "We have to stop this! We… have to eat, we have to—"

But he'd turned her around and was kissing her again,

his hands already finding their way under her top.

A loud ringing sound finally penetrated her befuddled brain.

"David," she mumbled against his lips, but he ignored her. "David," she said again and pushed against him. "Your phone is ringing," she tried again between kisses.

He finally lifted his head, his eyes molten chocolate.

Still breathing heavily, he looked for his phone and answered it. Dana turned back to the stove, just in time to save the omelet.

While he was talking, David walked toward the sliding doors that led to a small patio.

Dana quickly got out the plates, dished up the omelets, and put on the kettle. When David returned, they could sit down like two normal people and eat. She was starving. The last meal they had was lunch yesterday.

He was finishing his call, and she looked up as he walked toward her. Oh, her poor heart. She quickly looked around for something else to do—otherwise they were never going to get anything into their stomachs.

She pointed to his chair before he could come closer. "Sit, we're going to eat."

"Yes, ma'am."

"Eat before it gets cold," she ordered and sat down.

He took her hand and brought it to his mouth. "Thank you for cooking for me."

"It's frightening to cook for one of Rosa's sons, I can tell you."

He bit into the omelet and groaned. "I didn't realize how hungry I am—this is so good."

"Everything okay?" she asked, pointing to his phone.

"Yes. There's no big crisis, but I'll have to leave tonight. I was hoping to stay another night." He took her hand. "But we have an early meeting tomorrow, so it would make more sense to leave tonight."

"Of course." Dana tried to ignore the sudden hollow feeling inside of her.

He pulled his laptop closer while still eating. "But let's see if we can find out anything more from old newspapers." He grinned. "I have been trying to do this since early this morning, but you kept luring me back to bed."

Indignant, she gasped. "Me! You're the one who's insatiable," she blabbered before she could stop herself.

His eyes darkened. "You're right. But I'm not the only one, am I?" he asked and took her hand.

She wanted to disagree, but she picked up the touch of uncertainty beneath his smile. David Cavallo uncertain about something?

She lowered her gaze, confused.

"Am I?" he insisted, playing with her hand.

She had to be honest. "No, you're not," she agreed, but quickly pointed to his laptop. "How far back can you trace old newspapers?"

His eyes narrowed slightly, but then he pulled the laptop

closer with his other hand. "We should be able to find everything that was written two years ago. I don't think that will be a problem. And it's nice to know I'm not the only one who's insatiable."

It took a few seconds before she registered the last part of what he was saying.

"David…" was all she could get out, her blood heating again, her hormones going haywire.

"I know." His voice was soft as he gazed at her. Then he turned his head back toward the computer, her hand still in his. "Let's see what we can find out."

Chapter Eleven

S HE WAS UP early. David had left late the previous evening. Very late. And she should have been tired, she should have slept like a log, but she was way too hyped up.

What exactly was going on inside of her, she was too wary to try to figure out. For David, she was probably one in a line of many women. He was only helping her out of guilt. But did that didn't stop her heart from doing cartwheels or her hormones from encouraging her to think all sorts of ridiculous things. Here she was already planning what to make for dinner in case he came over next weekend.

Aargh! She had to stop! Nothing could come of this; she knew that.

Her phone rang. It was Caitlin.

"Hi, Dana. Are you okay? When you left on Friday, you were so angry. I wanted to phone earlier, but Rosa seemed to think you and David needed time to talk?"

Dana rolled her eyes. "Yes, I'm fine. And yes, I slept with David," Dana said. There was no use even trying to hide this from Caitlin. The minute she heard Dana's voice, she'd know something had happened between her and David.

Silence. Then the scream. Smiling, Dana held the phone away from her ear.

"What?" Caitlin shouted. "How come you moved so quickly from being angry with the man to going to bed with him? You were glaring daggers at him when you left here."

Dana sighed. "I'm not quite sure. He organized for us to go and see two financial advisors who knew my dad and then we had lunch and then…"

"It happened?" Caitlin giggled.

"Yes," Dana said, a giggle also escaping.

"And?" Caitlin wanted to know.

Dana tried to think of words to describe what had happened, but nothing that came to mind could begin to express what she'd experienced.

"That good, eh?" Caitlin teased.

"Oh, yeah." Dana sighed. "But before you jump to any ridiculous conclusions, I know nothing can come of it. I'm trying to sort out my life. He's helping me. That's it. This is just a temporary thing."

"And you're okay with that?"

"Not all of us are destined to find our soul mates like you and Zoe did," Dana said quietly. "I'm happy enough. I'd like to put this thing about my dad behind me, but to do that I need to know what really happened before I can go on with my life."

"Were you able to find out anything else from the financial advisors you've seen?" Caitlin asked.

"To tell you the truth, I'm even more confused, but yes, we did find out several things." She told Caitlin about the two conversations they had.

"So this Johnson guy thinks your dad's death might not be suicide? That it might have something to do with the laundering of money?" Caitlin asked.

"I don't know, but at least we now know for sure he wasn't selling the product, and he wasn't earning any commissions from Hastings."

"And what about Sam Jordan? How come he didn't end up in jail?"

"Well, there wasn't much on him in the newspapers, but according to Toby Johnson, his commission payments aren't traceable," Dana replied and told her about the poachers.

"Wow, this is sounding more and more like something out of a thriller. What does David think?"

"He has contacts and is going to find out when Sam Jordan bought the house in Kleinmond and for what amount. From there, he can follow the money. I think we should talk to Jordan again."

"Please, promise me you'll wait for David before you talk to anyone again? I don't like the sound of this man."

"You sound like your mother." Dana smiled. "But I have been doing things for myself for quite some time, you know?"

"I know. Talking about things, what about your car?"

"Well, if David had his way, I would have had a car already," Dana grumbled and told Caitlin about the car they'd seen on Saturday.

"But that's wonderful, Dana, why don't you—"

"I can buy my own car, thank you very much. But the price sounds right, and I like the car, so I'll give the guy a call later today."

"It's okay to lean on someone else every now and then, you know," Caitlin said. "Especially if you're sleeping with him." She giggled.

"I can't believe you said that!" Dana cried out, crossly. "That's exactly why I'll buy my own car. I'm not sleeping with him because he can get me things!"

"I know that." Caitlin laughed. "But men like to think they are in charge even if they're not."

"Well, I don't need a man to buy a car. I'm quite capable of doing it by myself."

"Okay, Miss Independent, let me know what you're getting!" Caitlin sang before they ended the call.

Dana scrolled down the contacts on her phone. There were two calls she wanted to make. One was to the car dealer and one was to her mother's financial advisor. She was going to take David's advice and talk to this guy to try and find out how bad her mother's financial situation really was.

DANA TOOK A deep steadying breath. "Let me get this straight. So what you're saying is that my mother gets a generous income. Every month."

"Yes, of course the exact amount is confidential, but what I can tell you is that your mother is well provided for, even if she lived to be a hundred."

"Thank you. I appreciate you taking the time to talk to me," Dana managed before her phone dropped from her fingers. She bent forward, feeling sick. How could her mother do this? She'd always tried to find an excuse for her mother's behavior, tried to explain away why her mother treated her so badly, but this time...

Why, then, would her mother constantly claim poverty, beg, and take her money? Did her brother know?

Her phone rang and, still shocked, she answered.

"Miss Roux? This is Barry Cox, the car dealer. You were at our showroom on Saturday. I'm phoning about the car you looked at."

"Oh... yes?" she said, her head still reeling from the news she had just received.

The man's voice droned on. She was going to phone George in Dubai. It should still be daytime over there. Surely he would know? But why hadn't he said anything?

"All you will pay for is the difference." Barry's voice finally penetrated her thoughts.

"What difference?" she asked.

Barry cleaned his throat. "Oh, dear. I wasn't supposed to say that, but..." He laughed nervously. "Let me bring the car, and we can finish the paperwork—"

"What difference?" she repeated coldly.

"Um… Mr. Cavallo is paying for half of the car and you—"

Dana ended the call and threw her phone on the coffee table. She felt light-headed. Someone had just pierced her heart with a sharp object. There was no oxygen in the room—why couldn't she breathe?

Her mother had been using her, taking her money even though she knew very well how little teachers were paid. And David had simply ignored what she'd said. What was she—chopped bloody liver?

How could he? She specifically told him she'd buy her own car—she didn't need his help.

The low price the salesman quoted was, of course, possible only because David was paying half! And she believed them, stupid idiot that she was.

She wiped her eyes and stared in amazement at her wet hands. She was crying.

FRUSTRATED, DAVID STARED at the phone. The salesman from Hermanus had just phoned him. The bloody idiot wasn't supposed to tell Dana that David was paying for half of the car. But, damn it all, he wanted to make sure she got a good car and wouldn't be driving around in a dilapidated number like the one she had.

"What did the phone do to you?" Darryn asked, looking

up from his computer.

"It's Dana... I..." he began but wasn't sure how to explain what had happened.

The office door opened and Don strolled in, a grin nearly splitting his face in two.

"I hear you're in trouble again." He slapped David on the back.

"What do you mean?"

"Dana and Caitlin were on the phone when I left. All I could make out was that you thought you could pay for half of Dana's car and she wouldn't find out. Dana is upset about something else as well, but I didn't catch that. You, my poor brother, have a lot to learn about these women." Don smiled sympathetically.

"Come again?" Darryn looked from Don to David. "What's going on that I don't know about?"

Don pointed at David. "He tried to pay for half of a new car for Dana."

"What are you guys drinking?" Darryn cried out. "Are you also falling for a woman?"

David frowned. "I haven't fallen for anyone; I'm trying to help her. I feel responsible for the bloody story that led to her dad's death, and I'm helping her to get to the truth."

"By paying for half of her car?" Don shook his head.

David rubbed his face. "She found out it was my story that led to her dad's death, and she was upset. Her car also broke down. I drove her back to Hermanus, we spent time together, and I—"

"Back up a bit." Don's eyebrows rose. "Define 'spent time together'—did you sleep with her?"

David grabbed his laptop. He had to get out of here and phone Dana. "Not that it's any of your business, but yeah, I did," he said and walked toward the door.

"Wait a damn minute," Don called out, and David looked over his shoulder at his brother.

All the mirth had gone from Don's face. "You know Dana is Caitlin's best friend? And you know how I feel about my wife?"

David nodded.

"If you mess with Dana, you mess with me. Is that clear?"

"Crystal." David snarled and stormed out of the office. Damn it all to hell! He was only trying to help.

THE FIRST FIVE times she didn't even answer the damn phone. The sixth time, she answered. Well, snarled, really.

"I don't need your money. I don't need your help. I don't need you to make deals for me. I don't need you. Stay out of my life!"

Before David could say anything, she'd cut the connection.

Frowning, he stared at the phone in his hand. Now what? He couldn't remember a woman hanging up on him.

Ever. What was he supposed to do now? Crawl back? Apologize? But he didn't do anything wrong!

Fed up with the whole business, he opened his laptop. He didn't have time for a woman who didn't want his help, who didn't need him. Work on the newly finished hotel near the Kruger National Park was nearly completed, and they would have to start their campaign promoting the place in earnest now.

Ten minutes later, he was still staring into space. With an oath, he opened the file he should have been working on.

Ten more minutes later, he realized he wasn't going to get anything done. He had to try and fix this thing with Dana. But how? He grabbed his phone and scrolled down until he found Caitlin's number.

Chapter Twelve

UPSET, DANA THREW her phone down and started pacing.

She'd known getting involved with a Cavallo, especially this particular one, was a mistake. But did she listen to her instincts? No, because her hormones had taken over! Why her brain stopped functioning when he was around, she had no idea—it had never happened to her before. But ever since he'd kissed her…

It was minutes later before she became aware that she'd stopped pacing and was touching her lips. Fed up with herself, she rolled her eyes and picked up her phone again.

A car. She had to find one today, because she wanted to drive to Sam Jordan again. He was the only one with all the answers. She now knew where he lived; she didn't have his cell phone number, but there was no reason why he wouldn't open the door for her.

The number of the car salesman should still be on her phone. Surely he would have something she could afford? She could, of course, borrow her mother's car, but she didn't want to talk to her yet.

For that conversation she had to be calm, and at the moment she was still so angry and hurt. Why would her mother take her money when she had more than enough of her own?

She closed her eyes while listening to the ring tone. Her dad had helped her when she'd bought her first car; he'd helped her with all those forms and done all the talking.

Sniffling, she wiped her clammy eyes. She missed him dreadfully. He was the only person on whom she could depend.

But now she was on her own, and she could buy a car. And, damn it, she didn't need a man to do this—how difficult could it be?

CAITLIN SIGHED AND patted the seat next to her on the couch. Irritated, David sat down. He'd been hoping for a quick answer on how to fix the thing with Dana, but if he was reading Caitlin correctly, it was not going to be that easy.

"You guys are used to buying your way into things. You pay people to do stuff for you, you pay people to work for you, you pay people. And it would seem, you pay women to be with you. We—and by we, I mean my sisters, Dana, and I—don't operate like that. It was something both Don and Dale had to figure out."

"I was just trying to help…" he began, frustration clawing at his insides.

"I know. And I think deep down Dana knows too. But she has other problems besides trying to figure out what happened to her dad…"

"What problems?" he interrupted.

"I don't want to discuss Dana's—"

Really worried now, he touched Caitlin's arm. "What problems?"

Caitlin looked at him, a small smile hovering around her mouth. "Why do you want to know?" she asked.

"I… I…" He couldn't find the right words. "What problems?"

Caitlin laughed. "I see." She nodded and patted his arm. "I'll tell you because you are my brother-in-law, and I know something now that you don't know yet—"

"Caitlin, what are you talking about? Tell me, what other problems does Dana have?"

"She has spoken to her mother's financial advisor."

"I suggested that she do that," he murmured.

Caitlin proceeded to tell him how Dana's mother had apparently constantly been asking for money, even though she had more than enough.

"Wow." He shook his head. "I can't even begin to understand what Dana must be feeling."

"And then on top of that news, she heard that you also disregarded her feelings and tried to pay for half her car."

"I didn't disregard her feelings—" he began hotly, but

realized that was exactly what he'd tried to do. "Okay, yeah, I can see why she'd think that. But that was not what I was thinking!"

"I know," Caitlin said in a placating tone.

He rubbed his face. "So how do I fix this?"

"You're halfway there if you understand how your actions made her feel."

David drove away from Caitlin and Don's house scowling. Damn it to hell! Understanding women was obviously not a skill a man was born with.

WEDNESDAY AFTERNOON SHE had her car. The salesman had kindly brought her two cars in her price range to test drive. She'd decided on one and felt quite good about herself.

After he assured her what he was doing was standard procedure, she felt better about leaving him to handle all the paperwork and registration. All she had to do was sign the final papers.

She'd done it all by herself. She hadn't needed David Cavallo. So why wasn't she feeling more triumphant about the whole thing?

She sat down on a chair at the kitchen counter. Because she missed him. He'd been in her little house, and everywhere she looked she could still see him, see his smile, remember the gentle touch of his hand on her back, his searing kisses…

Aarrgghh! This was not helping! She looked at her watch. It was still early enough to take the drive she was thinking about. She was not going to phone anyone and would just hope to find them at home.

She still had to confront her mother, but at this point talking to anyone else seemed a better option.

"WHAT THE HELL do you want now?" Sam Jordan snarled the minute he opened the front door. "I told you everything I know."

The big man was angry, but Dana was determined not to be intimidated.

She squared her shoulders. "I only need a few minutes of your time…" she began with a smile, but he started shutting the door.

"I don't have anything else to say to you." He proceeded to close the door.

Stunned, Dana put her hand out to stop the door. Why was he so angry? She only wanted to ask him a few questions.

"Can you tell me how the money laundering worked?" she managed to say and the door stopped a few centimeters from completely closing.

"Where did you hear about that?"

"Well, I also spoke to Toby Johnson…" she began, but Sam opened the door and pushed a thick finger under her nose.

"Don't mess with things you don't understand, little girl—go home." He snarled again and shut the door in her face.

Shocked, Dana stared at the front door for a few seconds. Gone was the affable man with his evasive answers she and David had seen last Saturday. Today, Sam Jordan was upset, angry, and, if she wasn't mistaken, he was threatening her.

Slowly, she walked back to her car. Toby Johnson had also tried to warn her when he'd said not everyone would like her asking questions about something that happened almost two years ago.

But, damn it, she had to know. She now had confirmation that her dad wasn't part of Hastings's scheme, didn't sell his product. But his death still remained a mystery. It couldn't have been suicide. She was even more certain of that than before.

But how did she prove it? Dejectedly, she got back in her car and drove away. She'd see whether Toby Johnson had anything else to add to his story.

It was another beautiful day, and the drive to Caledon should have been pure pleasure. But she was hurting. To find out her mother had used her, the guy she'd slept with had tried to dupe her—all in one day—was a bit much. And then, there was this constant need to prove her dad's innocence.

Hopefully she'd find more answers in Caledon.

A BRAND-NEW CAR was parked in front of the Johnson house. She didn't know much about cars, but this was a Mercedes. Caitlin drove one just like it. The Johnsons probably had a visitor.

For a moment, she was undecided. Maybe she should have phoned first. But, damn it, she was here. She needed to find out what else this guy knew. She got out and walked purposefully to the front door.

The door opened on her second knock. Toby Johnson stood there, the smile on his face vanishing quickly.

"What do you want?" he asked brusquely.

"I—" Taken aback, she stopped talking.

Something was very different from the last time she was here, but she couldn't quite put her finger on it. The television was blaring in the background, and she glanced inside the house before she spoke to him.

"I was hoping I could talk to you again about my dad," she began tentatively.

Before he could say anything, his wife appeared behind him and took his arm.

"My husband isn't well enough to talk to anyone today. Please leave," she said rudely and closed the door in Dana's face.

Flabbergasted, Dana stared at the door.

What... Turning back toward her car, she noticed the Mercedes again. As far as she could see, there hadn't been anyone else in the house.

Frowning, she got into her car and drove back. Pieces of a big puzzle tried to fall into place, but she felt like her head would explode, and she simply couldn't grasp the final picture.

All she wanted to do at that moment was go back to her house and try to figure out what was going on. But there was still one more stop she had to make before she would be able to sleep tonight. Her mother.

DAVID HEARD DANA'S voice floating through the open window as he was about to knock on her front door. He froze.

"Did you know about it?" she was asking.

Frowning, he listened to the one-sided conversation.

"I've just been to see her, and she eventually admitted she pleaded poverty so I would give her money," Dana was saying again, a hitch in her voice.

"I spoke to her financial advisor," she said, and David finally realized she had to be talking about her mother.

He shouldn't be listening. He knocked on her door.

"Just a minute," he heard her say, and the front door opened.

It was a completely different Dana from the one he'd left on Sunday night. There was no welcoming smile. Instead she was frowning, her red-rimmed eyes telling their own story.

And she was very, very pale.

"I don't want to see you," she said and tried to close the front door in his face, but he stepped forward, and in a huff, she turned her back on him, resuming her telephone conversation.

"I don't know. She said she'd pay me back, but..." Dana sat down on a chair and rolled her shoulders.

David's hands itched. He so badly wanted to go to her and massage her shoulders, but the fed-up glance she was sending in his direction warned him not to even try.

"She's our mother, so yes, at some point I will. But not right now. Okay, thanks." She put the phone down and looked straight at David.

"I don't want to talk to you," she said.

"Fine. Because I want to talk to you." David took the chair opposite her.

His fingers were tingling. He wanted to kiss her, hold her, make love to her, but before he could do that, he had to try and make amends. He had to fix this.

"I'm sorry about the car. It's just..." He got up and started pacing.

He had to get this right. No deal he'd ever done before had been so important. Words were his thing; he knew how to use them. They were well-known tools he arranged in very specific ways to entice people, to persuade them—but with Dana's big eyes on him he wasn't sure how he could apologize.

He turned to her, desperate to make her understand what his reasoning had been. "I want you to have a dependable car, one that won't leave you stranded," he said and pressed his hand against his heart. "I need to know you'll be safe. And if that means I have to pay for half your car, then that's what I'll do," he ended, hoping for a smile.

Dana jumped up, furious. Dejectedly, he rubbed his face. He obviously hadn't used the right words.

"If that's your idea of an apology, you have a lot to learn. I told you I'd buy my own car. But no, you had to be in charge; you had to do things your way. Well, I've got news for you—I don't need a big, strong man in my life to buy a car. There is one standing in my garage, which I bought all by my lonesome little self. You've done your bit, so you don't have to feel guilty anymore," she said, her eyes blazing even though her lower lip was quivering. She smiled bitterly.

David stared at her stubborn chin. Maybe now was not the time to tell her he and the salesman had spoken about the two cars they showed to Dana. He had to make sure she'd get a car in a mint condition.

"And," she said with a twisted smile, "you even got sex out of the whole business!"

The stab of pain went right to his heart. He stood up slowly. "It was much more than sex and you know it," he said quietly and tried to catch her eye.

But she refused to look at him. "Just go, David. I've had enough confrontation for one day." Sounding tired, she pointed toward the door.

Swearing under his breath, David strode to the door. There was no reasoning with her tonight. He'd sleep at Don's house and try again tomorrow morning to speak to her.

Just before he opened the door, he remembered and turned back to her. "I'm sorry about your mother."

She frowned. "How did you know?"

"Caitlin. I made her tell me, but I also heard you on the phone," he said honestly and pointed toward the window. "It was open."

"It's none of your business."

The stab of pain he'd just felt intensified. He opened the front door. She was right, of course. He felt responsible for her father's death, but whatever her mother did or didn't do wasn't his concern.

"I..." he heard her say and turned around.

With tired movements, she combed her fingers through her hair. "You were the one who suggested I find out what her situation is. Thank you for that. And it turns out it's great. Much better than mine, in fact," she murmured before turning around and heading toward her bedroom.

David stared after her for a few minutes. He had to force himself not to follow her and pick her up in his arms. This urge to protect, to wipe her tears, to prevent someone from hurting her was not something he'd experienced before.

Slowly, he closed the open window and made sure the

lock on her door worked before he closed it behind him. To see her like this and not be able to offer his help was ripping his heart out.

After he got into his car, he sat for a while, staring at Dana's house. What was it with this woman that he couldn't just walk away? Yes, he felt guilty; he wanted to find out what had really happened, but she obviously didn't need his help. So why was he sticking around?

He had information he wanted to share with her. It had been easy to find out Sam Jordan bought his house about eighteen months ago. That was one of the reasons he was here, but he could have told her that over the phone. Exchanging information was not why he was here, why he couldn't stop thinking about her, why he couldn't keep his hands to himself.

He drove away slowly. Images of Dana kept swirling around his head as if they wanted to tell him something. But he was too tired and feeling too dejected to make sense of what was going on inside of him.

She'd made her feelings clear—she didn't need him; she thought he was only after her for the sex.

Sex. That word again. But for the life of him, sex didn't begin to describe what had happened between them. Sex had the connotation of lust and, damn it, what he'd found in Dana's bed was way more than mere lust.

He opened his car window and welcomed the balmy sea breeze. But he was going to try again to make her listen to him. What did Caitlin say? Oh yes, he'd disregarded her feelings. Maybe he should use that line when he tried to talk to her again tomorrow.

Hopefully, he'd also have information about Hastings by then. According to newspaper articles, the guy had been sentenced to ten years in prison. But recent reports were saying he might qualify for early parole because of health issues.

David pressed the remote to open the gate to Don's house and drove into the garage. He also hoped he would get information about the whole money laundering scheme. But until then, he had time to try to figure out what he could say to Dana tomorrow.

Or he could just ignore the whole thing and drive back to Cape Town tonight. Never see Dana again except at family functions? Nope, he didn't like that idea. At all.

Chapter Thirteen

D ANA WOKE UP startled, her heart in her throat. Something had woken her. What had she heard? She cocked her head. There it was again. A noise coming from her front door.

Immediately furious, she got up and stormed to the front door. David bloody Cavallo. She was going to kill him. She flung open the door at the same time she switched on the front porch light.

But the porch was empty, the street silent. A chill crept up her spine, and she started closing the door. That was when she saw it.

WHAT THE HELL? David sat up in bed and glared at his phone. If this was one of his brothers ringing him this time of night, he was going to…

He picked up his phone. It was Don. Swearing, he answered.

"Do you know what time it is?" he barked into the phone.

"Where are you?" Don asked him. There was something in his voice.

"In Hermanus, why?" he asked, rubbing his face.

"Good. Go to Dana. Now."

It took a few seconds for David to understand what Don was saying. But then he was, grabbing his jeans and his keys.

"Why? What happened?" A cold hand clamped around his throat.

"I'm not sure. She just phoned Caitlin, but we couldn't quite make out what she was saying. Something happened to upset her enormously. Could you please go find out what's going on and let us know? We're leaving for Hermanus as soon as we've packed up."

"On my way." After hopping into his jeans, he sprinted for the door.

HE SAW IT as he ran up the porch steps. The front door flew open, and Dana stood there, her eyes big, her whole body shivering. There was a note, he saw, but for the moment that didn't seem important. He stepped over the body of a mutilated cat and had Dana in his arms before she could open her mouth.

She was shaking so badly she couldn't walk.

He locked the front door behind them and picked her up. Her arms went around his neck and she clung to him, sobbing against his chest. His own heart was beating furiously and with the adrenaline rush dying down, he sat down quickly with her in his arms. He was feeling dizzy.

He'd gotten there in record time—his only thought that something had happened to Dana. His breathing finally calming down, he pulled her closer, stroking her hair until she stopped sobbing.

"Can I get you anything?" he asked.

She shook her head, her arms folded tightly around his neck.

"What happened?"

"Something woke me up." She sniffed, sat up, and dropped her hands.

"I thought it was you on the porch, and I—"

"Wanted to take a swing at me?" He smiled and pulled her closer.

But she didn't return his smile. Another shiver shook her body. "And then I saw... that." She pointed toward the front door.

"There was a note," he said, remembering the piece of paper he'd seen. He put her down gently.

"A note? I just saw the dead cat and remembered..." Dana swallowed and, still shivering, wrapped her arms around herself.

He walked outside and picked up the note with two pens he found in his pocket. It was tucked beneath the cat.

"I noticed this when I came up the stairs." He placed the note on the coffee table in front of Dana.

She bent forward and read it. Catching her breath, she became even paler than before and sagged back against the cushions.

David had also been reading the typed letter. "You shouldn't be snooping around," the note read.

Dana looked stricken.

"What?" he asked urgently.

"I've been to see Sam Jordan and I immediately thought of him when I saw the dead cat."

Before he knew what he was doing, he had his hands around her upper arms and was lifting her up. "What?" he bellowed. "Are you completely crazy?"

Dana's eyes blazed, but her lower lip quivered. Swearing, he caught her to him. "Sweetheart, you can't go around asking questions on your own—these guys don't play around!"

"I know," she said. "But he was quite friendly last time when you and I were there. But then yesterday he threatened me, though I didn't think he'd actually do anything." She frowned. "Maybe it wasn't him, maybe it…"

David saw red. He took out his cell phone. "That's it, I'm calling the police."

DANA LEANED BACK against the cushions. She hadn't done anything, but she was exhausted. It was midmorning, and David had just closed the front door behind the detective.

Don was busy in the kitchen, cooking up something from all the bags they'd brought along. Caitlin was sitting next to her on the couch.

They had to wait about two hours before any police arrived and another hour for the tired-looking detective to make an appearance. They'd told him about the people they'd been talking to and about Sam Jordan's threat, but he seemed very skeptical.

"Were they able to find any fingerprints?" she asked tiredly.

"Maybe on the note—we'll have to wait and see. I'll help Don." He walked toward the kitchen.

Caitlin stroked her hair. "I still can't believe someone is trying to frighten you!"

"Well, I am frightened, all right, but I'm also more determined than before to find out what is going on."

"Will you please let Don and David help you?" Caitlin asked.

"I don't need—"

Caitlin put a hand on her arm. "Yes, you do. We all need people to help us at times. And you can't stay here. Let's pack a bag for you. You're coming to stay with us."

"It's really not necessary—"

"Yeah, it is," Don said from the kitchen. "I'm nearly done here. Go pack your bag, then we'll have lunch."

Dana wanted to say no, but she was too relieved to put up a fight. Her safe space had been violated. This had always been her happy place, but now she couldn't wait to leave. She'd be back in a few days, but for now it would be wonderful to get away from her mother, from her house, from whoever was trying to scare her.

"Are you still angry with David for trying to buy you half a car?" Caitlin asked when they reached Dana's room.

Dana sighed. "If you put it like that, it sounds so silly. But I found out about it right after I heard what my mother has been doing."

"He came to see me to find out how he could apologize."

"Apologize? He didn't apologize. He told me he wanted me to be safe, as if I can't look after myself."

"Well, at least talking about him has brought color back to your face." Caitlin giggled and opened the cupboard door.

Dana sighed and sat down on the bed. "He makes me so mad! But then there's a dead cat on my porch, and he comes storming to my rescue."

Caitlin took down a suitcase and put it on the bed. "Like a knight in shining armor!" She giggled again. She reached out and touched Dana's shoulder. "He's a good man, Dana. They all are, but I've always thought David the gentler one. And he is genuinely concerned for your well-being."

Dana groaned. "I know. But I was still recovering from the news about my mother when they called about the car, and when I heard what he'd done I just saw red. It was easier to be angry with him."

"You've spoken to your mother?" Caitlin asked tentatively as she began packing the suitcase.

Dana sighed. "Yes. Not that it was much use. She became hysterical and accused me of not wanting her to have nice things and heaven knows what else."

"I hope you're going to ignore that!" Caitlin cried. "That woman. I know she's your mother, but really, Dana, she is the most selfish person I know."

Shrugging, Dana stood up and listlessly threw things into the suitcase. "I just don't think I've been the daughter she wanted. Maybe I should have tried harder, maybe—"

Caitlin swore and pushed Dana back on the bed. "Now you listen to me. You are a beautiful, brave, strong woman. Your mother has problems; you don't—do you understand?"

"What's taking you so long?" David yelled, and they heard his footsteps approaching.

When he appeared in her bedroom doorway, Caitlin was finishing packing. "I'm telling Dana here how special she really is, but she seems to have a hard time believing that."

She closed the suitcase and put it on the floor. "You try and convince her; I'll help Don." She smiled and left.

David put his hands in his pockets and slowly walked closer. "It's true, you know," he said quietly. "The way you've managed to carry on with life after what happened to your dad is amazing. Not many people would have been able to cope."

"I always had Caitlin and her family." She picked up a pillow and hugged it close.

David bent down and loosened her hands from around the pillow. "And now you also have me. Will you please let me help you?" He pulled her up.

She looked at him, and her heart tripped.

Letting him get closer was eventually going to cause her more heartache, but at the moment she didn't care.

Leaning forward, she placed her hands on his upper arms, her head on his chest. He went very still before his arms folded around her.

"Was that a yes?" She heard the smile in his voice.

"Yes, that was a yes." She smiled. "I was rude to you last night and said things I didn't mean. I'm sorry," she said softly, her head still against his chest.

He was quiet for a moment. "Was that an apology?"

"Yes, I know how to apologize." She lifted her head.

David folded his hands around her face. "I can't promise that I will not try to help you again, because I will. I need to. But I promise to talk to you about it first, okay?"

She smiled. "See? That's not an apology!" she teased. "You should have..." she began, but his eyes darkened, and his mouth came down hard on hers.

And she forgot what she was going to say, forgot about the horrible experience of earlier, forgot she shouldn't be kissing this man, forgot why she ever thought that.

"Hey, you two!" Don shouted down the corridor. "We want to eat!"

David lifted his head, his eyes nearly black. "You go. I

need a few minutes."

She frowned, and he pulled her against his hardness. Her eyes widened.

"Now do you understand?" He growled.

Giggling, she fled.

Chapter Fourteen

S HE WAS TRYING to read when her phone rang. Sleep was very far away. Don and Caitlin had retired to their room hours ago, but she was still too hyped up from everything that had happened.

Caitlin had given her a copy of her mother's latest romance. Dana was hoping she'd be feeling sleepy by now, but the book was a bit steamier than any of the previous ones Caitlin's mom had written, and sleep was now even further away.

"You okay?" Dana heard David's voice in her ear, and she relaxed.

If she were to be honest, she'd hoped to hear from him.

"Yeah. I think so. Caitlin and Don have been so kind. I feel terrible that I've been such a nuisance."

David swore softly and she had to smile.

"You have such a way with words!" she teased.

"We'll do anything for you. Surely you know that?" He was clearly irritated.

Did he realize what he was saying? But before she could say anything else, he continued.

"With everything that happened today, I didn't get a chance to talk to you. Well," he said, and now she could hear the smile, "I kissed you, but we never talked."

She inhaled sharply. "David!"

"What? That's what happened, isn't it? That's what always happens when I'm around you. I turn into a randy teenager!" He was clearly not very happy with the idea.

"Well, then don't be around me," she joked, hoping to lighten the conversation, because she was suddenly feeling so hot.

It was quiet for so long, she thought he'd hung up.

"David?" she asked into the silence, sitting upright in the bed.

"What I wanted to tell you was that I was able to track down when Jordan bought the house in Kleinmond."

It took her a few second to realize he'd changed the topic completely. When his words finally penetrated finally penetrated her befuddled brain, she anxiously clutched the phone with both hands.

"Yes?"

"It was just after the trial. For six million South African rand. Exactly how he paid for it isn't clear, but what I do know is that he didn't take out a bond."

"Six million!" She breathed, her brain working overtime. "Where did the money come from, do you know?"

"I'm not quite sure, but I'm working on it. I've also made inquiries about Hastings. There were rumors he might be eligible for early parole because of his health. And apparently, he'll be out on bail soon."

"After only two years? What about all the millions that were lost?" Dana asked.

"Well, it is, of course, still a question—what happened to the money. As I've said before, there is a story here, one I'm determined to uncover."

His words sent a chill down her spine. She still had to tell him she'd also been to the Johnson house. "Please just promise me you'll be careful. I don't like the way these people operate. They seem to be a law unto themselves."

"Worried about me?" David asked.

Now it was her turn to be quiet. What should she call this strange concern for David's well-being? She couldn't bear the thought that anything bad might happen to him, that he might get hurt. In fact, her stomach churned when the thought about it.

"Dana?" he asked.

She could ignore his question like he had ignored hers. But he'd come to her today when she'd needed him. So she'd try to be honest.

"Yeah, I worry about you."

He inhaled sharply. "You know what you do to me when you say something like that?" He groaned.

Her eyes closed. The man's voice alone turned her insides to mush. It was a very good thing he wasn't next to her, or she would have jumped all over him.

"David ..."

"Can I take you out tomorrow night?" he asked.

"As in a date?"

He laughed. "Yes, as in a date."

She should say no. This had no future. There could be no happily ever after with him. What did a school teacher from Hermanus have in common with a hotel tycoon? The mere thought was ridiculous. He had his choice of beautiful women; he was merely toying with her.

"Just say yes. You don't have to analyze everything to death, you know."

"Okay, yes." There would be enough time afterward to cry about all the wrong decisions she'd made.

"I'll pick you up around seven? And Dana?"

"Yes?"

"I like being around you, so that's not going to change any time soon." And before she could utter another word, the line was dead.

She stared at the phone. Her whole body was tingling as if he'd been here, as if he'd touched her. Rolling her eyes, she flopped back on the bed. She'd been threatened today; someone had left a dead cat with a warning note on her porch. And what was the only thing she could think of in the middle of the night? David.

With a groan, she switched off her light. She might as well close her eyes. Reading about a hot hero with clever hands was not sleep inducing.

"YOU HAVE GORGEOUS legs—it's summer, show them off!" Caitlin smiled as she passed a tiny blue lace dress on to Dana. "Did David say where he was taking you?" she asked as she went through the dresses on the rail in a lovely boutique.

Dana took the dress. Caitlin in a shop was an unstoppable force—that Dana had discovered when they were still in school. From experience, Dana knew it was no use complaining. She just had to go with the flow. She didn't have to buy anything; these things were way more expensive than she could afford anyway, but she'd try them on.

Over breakfast, she'd told Caitlin David was picking her up tonight, and before she knew it, Donato had been dropped off with his grandma Rosa, and they'd hit the shops.

"Go try that one while I see if I can find anything else," Caitlin said while riffling through the clothes.

"As long as it's not shorter," Dana said and looked at the tiny piece of clothing on the hanger. It was a beautiful dress, but she didn't normally wear her dresses this short. She didn't normally have money to buy anything else besides clothes she could wear to work. This was definitely not something she could wear to class, and there was no way she would let David see her in this dress...

His eyes would darken and smolder, and he would draw her closer, touch her—

"Do you need any help?" a shop assistant asked nearby.

"Um, n-no," Dana stuttered and scurried away to try on the dress. The damn man wasn't even here, and she was getting all hot and bothered just thinking about him.

Minutes later, she stared at herself. Was that really her? She turned around to look at the back of the dress, and the curtain opened.

"Dana!" Caitlin cried out and opened the curtain wider. "You look absolutely stunning. This is it; you have to take this," Caitlin insisted.

For the first time Dana looked down at the price tag and groaned. "It's way too expensive," she said and pulled down the zipper. "I just bought a car, remember? And anyway, I have something I can wear. But it was lovely trying on all these beautiful clothes. I never get time to do this during the school term," she babbled.

Caitlin had a stubborn look on her face, but Dana was determined not to be persuaded. She had enough money to pay for the dress—that was, if she didn't eat for the rest of the month. And that was just plain silly.

"Let me get into my own clothes, and we'll go for coffee and cheesecake." She closed the curtain in front of Caitlin.

Caitlin was quite cheerful when they left the small boutique, and she took Dana's arm. Dana looked suspiciously at her friend. Caitlin didn't usually let go of something once she'd put her mind to it.

"Motherhood is good for you." Dana smiled and patted her friend's hand.

OF COURSE, THAT evening she realized why Caitlin had been so pleased with herself.

"I told you I can't afford the dress," she said exasperatedly and tried to hand it back to Caitlin.

"I know. And it's not your dress; it's mine. I'm lending it to you, like I've done a thousand times before." Caitlin smiled broadly.

Dana stared at the dress. She was wearing one of the dresses Caitlin had packed for her and had just been thinking how much nicer she had looked in the blue one she'd tried on when Caitlin knocked on her door. And here was the dress.

"Come on," Caitlin cajoled, pulling down the zipper of the dress Dana had on. "I even have shoes to match," she said excitedly.

Dana wanted to be angry, but Caitlin's enthusiasm was contagious and within minutes she was dressed in the blue number.

"Sexy dress plus killer heels." Caitlin giggled, handing her a pair of exquisite shoes.

Dana stared at the beautiful pair of blue sandals in the exact same color as the dress. In awe, she touched them. "They're beautiful, but where did you get them?"

"Just something I picked up later today. Aren't they beautiful?" Caitlin breathed. "Come, we wear the same size. You can be the first to wear them."

"Caitlin, really, I have shoes," she said crossly.

"I know, but you're only borrowing these—what's the harm in that?" Caitlin smiled.

Dana sighed and took the shoes from her friend. "I know manipulation when I see it," she grumbled but put on the shoes. They were, of course, a perfect fit and looked gorgeous with the dress.

"Dana! Caitlin!" Don called from downstairs. "David's here!"

"Come on, I'll comb your hair, and you still need lipstick. I can't wait to see David's face when he sees you in this."

Dana stared at her reflection for a few seconds.

This was all just make-believe. Tomorrow morning she'd wake up, the shoes and dress would be gone, and she would go back to her normal life.

"Thanks, friend. But please remember, this is just a dinner date. David is helping me because he still feels guilty about my dad. As soon as he has unraveled the story, he'll move on to the next woman—you know that; I know that."

"I know nothing of the sort. From what I've seen so far, he can't keep his eyes or hands off you. Come on, you look beautiful!" she sang and pulled Dana out of the room.

"DRINK?" DON ASKED but David shook his head. "No, thanks, I'll be driving," he said and looked toward the top of the stairs where Dana would appear any minute now.

Don laughed and slapped him on the back.

"You've got it bad, man," he said and poured a glass of wine for himself.

David shrugged. "I don't know what you're talking about."

Don pointed toward the stairs. "You've been staring at those stairs ever since you arrived." He cocked his head. "You got a thing for our Dana?"

David frowned. "No one's got a thing for anyone. I'm helping her find out what really happened with the Hastings case. As you very well know, I feel I owe it to her. I'm taking her for a meal. That's all there is to—"

A movement on the stairs caught his eye, and there was Dana. Something hit him in the gut—hard. A gasp escaped before he could prevent it. She looked gorgeous and sexy as hell. Pale blue lace gently hugged her generous breasts, fitted perfectly over the rest of her body, and ended high above her knee, leaving her gorgeous legs bare.

His fingers tingled, and before he knew it, he was standing at the bottom of the stairs, holding out his hand to her. She descended, one step at a time, and he noticed the shoes. He was a dead man. The high heels made her legs look even longer, even sexier.

Don barked out a laugh, but David ignored it. Caitlin called out a greeting, and he nodded but his eyes never left Dana.

A small smile hovered on her lips when she reached the bottom of the stairs.

"You look amazing." He bent down. He simply had to kiss her.

He swallowed the small gasp on her lips and pulled her closer.

"Well, are you two sure you want to go out?" Don asked behind him. "We have a few empty rooms upstairs."

David kissed Dana again. "Yes, we're going out." He pulled Dana's hand through his bent arm.

Chapter Fifteen

WHEN DANA SLID into the small sports car, she was still trying to get her breathing under control. She'd always thought a man in a white shirt was nice, but nice didn't begin to describe David Cavallo wearing one.

He looked sexy as sin, and she had to force herself to look in front of her when he got into the car. She didn't want to be slobbering over him even before they left. Then he closed the car door, and his scent wrapped around her, caressing her skin.

"I made a reservation at an Italian place in Camp's Bay. It's not far from my place in Fresnay. We could have a nightcap there afterward if you like," he said as they drove away.

She gulped. A nightcap at David's place. The immediate images those words conjured up were black satin sheets and entwined, sweating bodies.

And, oh, hell, he was still talking but she hadn't been listening after "nightcap."

"What you eat?"

"Sorry?" she asked. "I..." She swallowed quickly.

He took her hand in his. "I'm asking what you like to eat. I know you like Italian food—I've seen you enjoy my mom's food, but what else?"

"Oh, I love food. I'm easy, I—I mean…" She stuttered when she realized how her words sounded.

David laughed and lifted her hand to kiss her fingers. "I know what you mean." He smiled. "But I have to differ— you might be easy when it comes to food, but I had to use all my skills to get you into bed!"

"David!" She gasped. "Don't say things like that!" She quickly turned her head to stare out the window, feeling the blush creeping up her neck.

"It's true. I've been wanting to get you into bed ever since I first saw you in my mother's restaurant, but you wouldn't even look at me," he teased.

"I looked—" she started indignantly.

"Yeah?" He smiled. "Not that I remember."

"I…" she began then closed her mouth. She couldn't tell him she couldn't look at him—her poor heart was out of control just being near him.

"It's true, you know." This time the smile was gone. He glanced in his rearview mirror before turning onto the lovely road that would take them along the sea toward Camp's Bay.

"What's true?" Her brain was completely muddled by his nearness. She didn't know what he was referring to. Her hormones had taken over her brain, and following their conversation was impossible.

He parked in front of the restaurant and looked at her, her hand still in his. "That I wanted you the minute I saw you. I didn't know it at the time, but when I kissed you at Zoe and Dale's wedding, I..." His voice dropped and he bent forward. "Knew," he whispered, just before his lips folded over hers.

Her head fell back against the soft leather of the headrest, her hands clutched the cool seat beneath her. David's lips caressed and stroked until she completely forgot where they were. All that mattered was that he didn't stop.

He lifted his head, his eyes smoldering, just like she'd thought they would earlier today. To her amazement, her fingers were in his hair. She didn't remember putting her arms around his neck.

David inhaled slowly and opened his door. "I promised you food, so let's go and eat." He quickly got out of the car.

Dana had a few seconds to compose herself before he opened the door on her side of the car. The dress slid up her leg as he helped her out, and his eyes dropped to watch as she pulled the dress down.

Then she was standing next to him. He pulled her close and groaned in her ear. "You're a knockout in this dress, but all I can think about is what you are wearing underneath."

Flames ignited just below her skin and threatened to engulf her whole body.

"I'll show you later," she whispered and shuddered as his eyes darkened.

Groaning, he dropped another flaming kiss on her lips before he took her hand. On unsteady legs, she followed him. When did she change into a flirt? She couldn't believe she'd blatantly invited him to look at her underwear. Well, the very little of it there was…

Another car parked just as they entered the restaurant. A Mercedes like the one Caitlin was driving. Like the one…

David put an arm around her and ushered her into the restaurant. His hand landed on her naked back, and she forgot everything else around her. The heat from his hand had her heart jumping up and down. How was she going to survive this dinner? Her mouth was dry as dust. She couldn't eat a thing.

They were shown to a table out on the big porch overlooking the sea. Although it was eight o'clock at night, this time of year the sun was still low on the horizon so they would be able to enjoy the usual spectacular sight of the sun setting over the Atlantic Ocean.

David talked to the waiter and pulled his chair close to hers. When his hand landed on her leg, the last oxygen left her body.

"David," she whispered.

"Are you cold?" he asked in a low voice.

She shook her head. Cold? She didn't think she'd ever be cold again. It would be a miracle if she didn't burst into flames any minute.

His fingers caressed her leg for another minute while his

eyes kept hers prisoner. Then he took his hand away and grabbed one of the menus.

"Let's…" He cleared his throat. "Let's order food. I've asked for a bottle of champagne; it should be here any minute. What would you like? Pasta? Veal? Steak?" He handed her the other menu.

Her fingers touched his as she took the big menu from him, and the heat from his fingers nearly scorched her. She clutched the menu in both hands. Because that was the only way she could think of to keep her hands to herself. What she wanted to do was not something that could be done in a public restaurant.

She tried to focus on the menu, but the letters kept jumping up and down. Fed up with herself and her raging hormones, she handed the menu to him.

"You can order for me. Anything." Realizing how desperate she sounded, she turned her head to stare over the sea.

The waiter brought the bottle of champagne and David talked to him while he poured the bubbly into their glasses. She was behaving like a sex-starved spinster. Why couldn't she calm down? What was wrong with her?

DAVID TRIED TO focus on giving the order to the smiling waiter. The guy's eyes kept darting in Dana's direction, and David had the primitive urge to put his fist in the man's face. He curtly gave the order and waited for the guy to leave. And felt immediately contrite. The poor man was just doing what came naturally.

He turned to look at Dana. She was resting her chin on her hands, looking out over the ocean. For minutes, he stared at her while images from the other day started swirling around in his head again, trying to tell him something.

She looked at him and smiled. His heart tripped before it began beating at a frantic pace. The overwhelming need to have this woman was staggering. He'd never wanted anyone with this kind of urgency before.

As if reading his mind, her smile trembled and her lips opened slightly. His hand landed on her leg under the tablecloth again, and he moved even closer to her. His fingers caressed her inner leg, and her breathing became labored.

"David," she whispered and licked her lips.

His hand slipped under her dress, and for a minute hovered over her heated core.

Her pupils dilated, and he swore softly.

Removing his hand from under the table, he pulled her head closer and branded her lips with a kiss.

"I want you. So badly." He growled. "But I promised you dinner." His breathing was shallow. He lifted his champagne glass, waited for her to do the same.

"To a beautiful night." Without taking his eyes off of her, he took a sip.

"It is a beautiful night," she agreed and looked out over

the sea again. "Look, the sun is just setting," she whispered and touched his arm.

The last rays of the sun caressed her face, leaving her glowing for a minute. His heart stumbled and he swallowed. His body felt too small to accommodate the powerful emotions swirling inside of him.

"Beautiful," he whispered, but his eyes hadn't left her face.

HOW SHE'D MANAGED to eat one morsel of food would always be a mystery to Dana. By the time they'd reached David's house, she'd virtually stopped breathing. All she could hear was the roaring of her heated blood in her ears.

David had put her hand on his leg and kept it there throughout the drive to his house. He'd said it was a short drive, but she was burning up. Where the hell was his house?

Finally, the road cleared in front of them, and he stepped on the gas. His sports car shot forward.

"How much farther?" she asked and knew she sounded like a petulant child.

David barked out a laugh. "Too damn far. I can't wait to get my hands on you, all over you, under you, in you!"

"David…" She gulped, feeling feverish and not sure how to convey it. Her hand slid up his leg.

"I want to get you there in one piece." He grunted, but gave her hand a squeeze before putting both hands back on the wheel.

By this time, her heart was beating so loudly, he had to be aware of it too. Desire like she'd never known before raged through her, and she held on to the seat with both hands.

DAVID OPENED THE car door for Dana and looked his fill at her long legs as he helped her out. And then she was in his arms, their mouths fused together. The earth beneath his feet rocked, the blood roared through his veins, and a basic, primitive instinct took control.

Without taking his mouth from hers, he backed her up against the car, his only thought to become part of her as quickly as possible. His fingers became entangled in her hair, and he dragged her head back, moving his mouth feverishly over her face, down her soft chin until he could bury his face in her throat.

He slid his hands down her sides, her shudder echoed through him, and his fingers found the hem of the short dress that had been taunting him all night.

With one movement of his arms, he shoved the material up over her hips so he could touch her.

She whimpered and moved her body against his, showing him what she wanted. He ran his fingers over her flat belly, slipped them beneath satin to find her hot and wet for him.

His knees buckled, and he leaned forward into her. When her legs opened, he stepped closer, pulled her body flush with his. She raked her fingers over his upper body and pulled at his shirt.

She groaned in frustration, lifted her head, and plucked at the buttons.

He tried to laugh but she sent him a searing glance, and the next minute buttons popped and flew to the ground.

That was all he needed to send him completely over the edge. Their mouths met again—hot, wet—and her tongue met his thrust for thrust. He struggled to find her heat again with his fingers, this time not succeeding in getting past the satin and lace barrier.

Grunting, he lifted his head and with one movement ripped the barrier that kept him from her. Her eyes widened, and she stilled for a millisecond.

He waited, waited.

With a determined thrust of her chin, her hand moved to his belt.

"Help me," she commanded.

"With pleasure." He grinned and quickly loosened his belt.

Without taking her eyes off of his, she shoved his pants down and lifted her legs around his body.

He was so ready for her, had been ever since he saw her coming down the stairs and had been this way all through dinner. Moving forward, he held her against the car and with one push he found his way home.

Her heat surrounded him like a glove. He caught her sob in his mouth and that was when he knew she was the one. This woman here in his arms was the one who had somehow managed to touch him so deeply that he would never be the same. She'd touched his very core. He loved her. It was that simple.

DANA COULDN'T THINK, couldn't breathe. She could only feel—David's warm, caressing hands on her skin, his breath on her face, his body throbbing deep within her. If she lived to be a hundred, she'd never forget this exact moment.

He lifted his head, his eyes liquid chocolate.

Amazed, her heart lifted, hovered uncertainly in the space between seconds before balance was attained and equilibrium found with a soundless click.

And she knew. She loved. Loved with everything she had, loved deeply, irrevocably, forever. David Cavallo had captured her heart, her soul, her very being. And even though this would never last, she'd always have this exquisite moment in time.

He began to move and she pulled him closer to her. Was it even possible for one's senses to accommodate so much emotion?

Tears threatened to spill over, and she buried her face in his neck, breathing in his scent. He increased his pace, and she willingly let herself be whirled away with him to a place far beyond the stars where time and place and logic didn't exist.

DEEP IN THE night, huddled against David's warm body, a memory nudged at her. She tried to make sense of what she was remembering, but then David pulled her closer, and she forgot everything else.

Chapter Sixteen

THE MOMENT SHE opened her eyes, she felt it. Something had changed. Everything was different. She was different. Because she loved.

Dana sat upright and looked down at her naked body. Groaning, she buried her face in her hands. She couldn't believe the things she'd done last night! Giggling, she pulled the sheet up under her chin and looked around the spacious room.

They'd eventually reached the bedroom. But not before they'd tried the dining room table, the couch in the living room, the wall in the corridor—she'd never have thought she could be this ... this ... adventurous!

A movement at the door caught her eye, and there he was. Leaning against the door, wearing only a pair of jeans, the man who'd stolen her heart. His hair was mussed, his eyes still sleepy.

Her hormones sprang to attention. Her heart did its usual crazy dancing, and before she knew what she was doing, she'd thrown off the sheet.

With two strides, David was with her, but this time, she

pulled him down, shoved him over on the bed, and straddled him before he quite knew what was happening.

Grinning, he looked up at her, gliding his hands up and down her legs. "I wanted to ask you if you were okay, but I can see I don't have to be worried."

"No, you don't. But you should be worried." She spread her hands out over his chest.

"Yeah?" He smiled.

"Yeah." She bent her head down. "Very worried."

HE WAS IN the kitchen, when he felt her. He looked up. She was blushing as she walked closer to him. He'd phoned Caitlin last night to let her know Dana would be spending the night, and then early this morning Caitlin had sent a message to say Don had left a bag for Dana on David's porch.

And a bloody good thing. Otherwise she would have worn the blue dress again, and he would have known she wasn't wearing anything underneath it, because he'd ripped her panties to shreds.

Swearing under his breath, he turned his back on her, switching on the coffee pot. He was in love, and he wanted to shout it from the rooftops, phone everyone he knew and tell them. But Dana was going through an emotional time; the last thing she needed now was some idiot declaring his love for her.

He would have to play it cool, give her time to get used to him, and wait until this whole mess surrounding her father's death was resolved before he could tell her how he felt.

"Coffee?" he asked coolly.

It was quiet behind him. He glanced at her over his shoulder. She'd cocked her head and was looking at him, frowning.

"What?"

"What's gotten into you?" she asked.

"Nothing, why?" he asked and turned back to the coffee machine.

Silence again. This time, when he turned around, she'd taken out her phone and was punching in numbers.

"What are you doing?" he asked and hurried over to her, She wouldn't look up at him and turned her back on him when he was close.

"I'm phoning Caitlin to come and pick me up," she said in a clipped voice and lifted the phone to her ear.

He grabbed it and ended the call.

"What are you doing?" she cried out, her eyes suspiciously bright.

Were those tears?

"You don't have to phone Caitlin. I'll take you home." Why the hell was she upset?

She made a grab for her phone but he held it above his head.

"David!" she called out. "My phone, I…" A tear escaped and rolled over her cheek.

Angrily, she wiped it away and whipped around. "Fine. Then I'll walk." She sniffed and marched toward the front door.

David stared at her for a few seconds before his brain registered what she was doing.

With two strides, he reached the door before her and moved in front of it.

"David—" she began, and another tear slipped onto her face.

Frowning, David pulled her closer. "What the hell is going on? Why do you want to phone Caitlin to pick you up? What happened between last night and now?" he growled.

"You tell me!" she nearly shouted. "This morning you—" She hiccupped and wiped a hand over her eyes. "This morning and last night, you couldn't get enough of me and now you… you don't even want to look at me!"

"That's not true!" he shouted, upset because she was crying, upset because he wasn't quite sure what exactly was going on.

She sniffled, wiped her face before looking him straight in the eye. "If you've had enough of me, you can tell me," she said, just a slight tremor still audible in her voice. "I'm a big girl; I can take it. I've always known this couldn't last. But I didn't think you'd be too much of a coward to tell me to my face."

And suddenly he was the hell in. This damn woman had him all tied up in knots and now she wanted to tell him what he was feeling as well. "Oh, you've always known, have you? And why is that?" he asked.

She rolled her eyes. Rolled her eyes! "Because, David, I'm a school teacher from Hermanus; my dad was in jail. You are a Cavallo; you probably have more money than you know what to do with. I know I've only been a temporary diversion for you. One that you are now clearly over. Let's leave it at that," she said in a cold voice and tried to move past him to the front door.

He was so astonished at the drivel she was talking he was speechless for a number of seconds. But then he saw her eyes, bright with tears, and a sliver of hope had him swallowing a grin.

Before she could open the door, he turned her around and backed her up against the door.

"So why are you upset?" he asked.

It was obvious this wasn't a question she'd been expecting.

"Wh-what do you mean?"

He combed her hair back with his fingers and trailed the back of his hand down her beautiful face.

"It's a simple question, Dana," he said and cupped her face with both hands. "Why does your idea that you've only been a diversion for me upset you?"

Her breath hitched in her throat; her gaze roamed uneasily over his face. But then her stubborn chin lifted. "It's not my idea."

"Then whose is it, because it's sure as hell not mine. Damn it to hell, Dana, I bloody love you!" he shouted.

She stilled in his arms. Her eyes shot open wide. For long minutes they stared at each other, their breaths coming out in gasps.

"What did you say?" she breathed, her eyes narrowing.

He smiled and dropped his hands. "You heard me."

She inhaled tremulously. "Could you repeat it? Please?"

"Why?"

"Because I love you too." A tiny smile was hovering on her lips.

His heart stopped. Just stopped. His breath came out in a whoosh. His hands landed on her shoulders. "What did you say?"

"You heard me." She mimicked his words of just now and smiled saucily up at him.

"Dana, damn it, tell me!" he roared.

"David, damn it, tell me!" She giggled.

"I love you!" they shouted together.

And then the wonder of it all settled in her eyes, and he knew for sure. He'd found his soul mate, the love of his life.

DANA COULD ONLY stare at David. So this was what happened when someone found their one true love. Her ditzy heart bounced around, out of oxygen for a few seconds before it finally settled in a new space where it fitted perfectly. Right next to David's.

Pure joy like she'd never experienced before rushed through her, bursting out in a laugh. She touched his face, traced the outline of his lips with her fingers, followed the line of his strong jaw down to his throat before she moved into him, folded her arms around him, and rested her face against his chest.

He lifted her chin with his finger, his eyes smoldering. And the passion was back, her blood heating within seconds. When he scooped her up as if he was Rhett Butler, she laughed helplessly and folded her arms around his neck.

Chapter Seventeen

DANA AND CAITLIN had been giggling and whispering in the kitchen for the past half an hour. Caitlin had phoned around lunchtime, asking when Dana was coming back. Of course, then he had to tell her that Dana would be staying with him, and then she had to talk to Dana, and here they were, having a glass of champagne in the middle of the afternoon.

Don lifted his glass. "So, it turns out you do have a thing for our Dana."

"Yeah," David grinned unabashedly. "I do. It's taken me all this time to figure it out, though."

"Well, make sure you talk to Dale. There is one more thing you need to discover, but I'll leave it to him to tell you," Don said.

In the background, Dana's phone rang. "What thing? I don't need to discover anything else. I love Dana. For me, she's the one. I don't need to know anything else."

"Talk to Dale, he—" But Don interrupted himself and stood up quickly, glancing over David's shoulder.

David turned around. Dana and Caitlin were approaching but something was obviously wrong.

Caitlin had her arm around Dana, and Dana…

"What the hell…" David jumped up and rushed over to them.

Dana was pale and near tears.

Alarmed, he pulled her into his arms and looked at Caitlin. "What happened?"

"She got a phone call from the police in Hermanus…" Caitlin began, and a shudder went through Dana's body.

He pulled her even closer.

"They've broken into my house, David," Dana cried brokenly. "The police said—" she began, but she choked and buried her face against him.

Caitlin moved closer to them. "Her house has been…" She swallowed and placed her hand against Dana's back. "It's been trashed." A tear rolled down her cheek.

Don joined them and pulled Caitlin into his arms.

"Who? Why?" David barked out.

Dana lifted her head and wiped her face. "They don't know whether anything has been stolen. I… have to go back to see if anything is missing."

"I'll go…" David began fiercely, anger making him shake.

But Don shook his head. "Dana is the only one who will be able to tell what, if anything, has been stolen," Don said.

David nodded, his brain working overtime. Was this linked to Dana's dad? If so, who would do something like this? Could it be Sam Jordan? Too blatant, he thought, for someone like the smooth Jordan. But who the hell else?

THEY WERE NEARING Hermanus when Dana remembered what had been bothering her for the past day.

"That's what I remembered," she murmured.

David was slowing down, because they'd entered the outskirts of the town. "What did you remember? When?" he asked.

"Last night. Something was bothering me, and I nearly remembered but then you…"

Grinning, he looked at her. "What? Had my way with you again?" he said and wiggled his eyebrows.

She giggled and touched his arm. It was still so wonderful to be able to do that, to see how he loved her touching him, how his eyes darkened in immediate response.

Sighing, she forced herself back to what she'd remembered. "I haven't told you," she began tentatively and quickly looked at him. He was so not going to like this, but she would have to tell him. "But when I went to see Sam Jordan, I also visited Toby Johnson again."

"What?" David cried out, nearly turning the wheel in the wrong direction. Swearing, he brought the car back into the road. "Why?" he barked as he turned onto her street.

"Don't shout at me!" She folded her arms.

David stopped in front of her house and turned to her,

breathing heavily. "Damn it, Dana! You should have told me. I... you..." Obviously exasperated, he pulled her closer. "You'll be the death of me yet. I don't mean to shout, sweetheart, but you scare me when you do things like that." The hands that were stroking her back weren't quite steady. "These are very bad people."

Contrite, Dana looked up at him. "I'm beginning to understand, and I'm sorry. I was angry with you for wanting to buy half a car for me. I was angry with my mother. My life seemed such a mess. This was one thing I was hoping to solve."

"Please don't do something like that again, okay?"

Smiling, she nodded. It was nice to have someone who worried about her.

"Okay, so you went to see Johnson. What did you remember about your visit?" David wanted to know.

Dana frowned, trying to remember. "A brand-new Mercedes was parked in front of his house. I thought they had visitors, but when he opened the door, I didn't hear any other voices."

"Back up a bit, you said he opened the door?" David frowned. "But the other day he looked so ill."

"Exactly. You were so right. I think it was all an act. Granted, I wasn't there very long, but the wheezing and coughing were gone. Also, and this is what I remembered last night, from where I was standing at the front door, I could look into the living room. The television was on. And it was a new one, you know, one of those thin, sleek numbers. I then also remembered that the first time we were there, the place looked dilapidated, but the dining room table was brand new. How can someone who can't even afford medicine have a new dining room table and a brand-new television?"

David stared at her for a few minutes, his eyes showing the rapid workings of his mind.

"I'm trying to get this straight. He told us about Hastings's scheme, about the money laundering, about his own involvement with Hastings, about Sam Jordan who didn't like the fact that your dad wanted to report Hastings's dealings. And he pretended to be very ill. Why?"

Dana nodded.

He snapped his fingers and then grabbed Dana's hand. "How can we find out which client told your dad about Hastings's dealings?"

Dana frowned and slowly shook her head. "I don't know that I can. Maybe my mother's financial advisor might know something? He and my dad were good friends."

"Maybe we should try to talk to him and find out if he knows anything."

Dana took out her phone and scrolled down, looking for the advisor's number. "His name is Grant Simpson. I'll see if I can get hold of him."

Behind them, a police car stopped.

"I'll talk to them while you see what you can find out

from your dad's friend." He got out of the car.

Dana turned to stare after him and sighed. She didn't know whether she was still dreaming, but if she was, it was one she hoped would never end.

"Simpson," the voice answered.

She wasn't quite sure why David wanted to talk to Simpson, but she'd try to set up an appointment for them to see him.

DISMAYED, DANA STARED at her trashed home. Everything that could break was broken. Food had been taken out of the cupboards and strewn over the kitchen floor. She felt like crying. Her lovely home, her safe place—she'd never be able to call it that again.

Behind her, David swore softly. "What a mess." He took out his phone. "I have the number of the people who usually clean Don's house. I'm phoning them to come and help."

"It's not necessary…" she began, but he was already talking to someone.

Fed up, she waited until he'd finished. "I said it's not necessary. I can do it myself."

"I know." He pulled her closer. "But you don't have to. You can supervise."

Dana tried to pull out of his hold. "I am quite capable of doing things for myself, David. Just because I love you, doesn't mean that I'm now suddenly helpless."

He threw a hand up in frustration. "I know that, damn it. But because I love you, I want to help you. All that money I have that I don't know what to do with? Well, here is something I can do with it. I can help you. I want to help you, because I love you. Can you understand that?"

Dana stared at him for another second before she laughed.

Grunting, he pulled her closer and landed a hard, wet kiss on her lips. "Anyone ever told you how difficult you can be?"

"I'm not difficult," she whispered against his mouth. "I'm easy, remember?"

"Oh, yeah." He grinned and kissed her again.

Her phone rang and, reluctantly, he let her go. It was Grant Simpson. He'd said he'd let her know about seeing them tonight.

Chapter Eighteen

DAVID DROVE AWAY from Grant Simpson's house, his thoughts racing through his head. It was already nearly eight o'clock, and he couldn't wait to tell Dana what he'd found out.

Simpson had agreed to see them that night, but Dana had to stay behind to show the cleaners where everything should go. She wanted to come with him, but she also didn't want to leave her place while someone else was there. And he missed her.

Desperately.

His phone rang. It was his mother. Grinning, he answered. Either Don or Caitlin or both probably told her he and Dana were in love.

"I'm just amazed it took you so long," he greeted her.

"You could have told me first," she scolded, but he could hear the smile. "What I want to know is why it took you so long to finally realize you're in love with Dana. I could have told you that after your first meeting."

"What do you mean?" David asked, amazed.

"The first time the Sutherlands came to lunch at Rosa's,

I noticed the way you looked at her. It was the same look I've seen on your father's face for the past nearly forty years when he looks at me."

David's breath caught in his throat, and he had to swallow a few times. "I didn't know then how I felt about her. I've always wanted what you and Dad have, you know? And I've been looking for someone who would touch my being, my core. And I've finally found her, Mom."

His mother sniffed. "Now you have me in tears, and I still have a restaurant full of people to cook for. Bring her home, will you? We like your Dana. Your father says she has spunk."

David smiled. That she had. In spades.

DANA SMILED AND turned around. The cleaners had just left and everything that hadn't been broken had been put back into place. She was still so angry at whoever did this. Hopefully, David would have some answers when he returned. He'd been very vague about why he wanted to talk to Simpson about her dad's client.

And strangely, she wasn't nearly as upset about her trashed house as she would have been a few months ago. This had been her haven, her happy place for so long, but now she'd found another place she'd rather be, another very happy place—with David. Now home was with him.

He hadn't said anything about marriage, and that was

fine, she realized surprised. For so long, she thought she'd never meet someone who could love her, who'd want to be with her. Her mother hadn't ever been happy with her, so why would anyone else? She'd always dreamed about finding that someone, though, the one who would know all there was to know about her but love her anyway. And now she had. Or rather, he'd found her. She wanted to be with him. Full stop. Nothing else mattered.

She heard footsteps on the porch and ran toward the front door. David would be so happy to see that the place had been put back into order.

Smiling, she switched on the porch light and opened the door. But it wasn't David who was standing there.

SIMPSON'S HOUSE WAS on the opposite part of Hermanus from Dana's house. The traffic was ridiculous, as it usually was with only a few days till Christmas. He should phone Dana to let her know he was on his way.

Swearing at a motorbike that cut in front of him, he dialed Dana's number. But it only rang and rang. He frowned. That was strange. By now the cleaners should be gone, and she'd be alone. There was no reason why she shouldn't hear her phone.

He looked for another number on his phone, stepping on the gas. Something was very wrong; he could feel it. He'd always trusted his instincts and they were screaming at him at the moment.

"GOOD EVENING, MR. Johnson, I wasn't expecting you." Dana tried to sound cool but she didn't like the way he was looking at her.

He rocked on his heels, his eyes bloodshot. "I tried to warn you." He looked over his shoulder to the quiet street. When he turned back to her, his mouth was twisted.

With a shove, he pushed her into the house and closed the door behind him. "You should have listened; you should have been scared after the dead cat. You came to see me again; you kept stirring. I trashed your house, but you keep stirring. I'm not going to jail, and you would have put me there."

He was wearing gloves, she saw. Gloves in December? Dana stared at the man in astonishment, a chill running up and down her spine. He was going to hurt her. She could see it in the way he moved; she could see it in his eyes.

Her phone rang from inside her room.

He advanced, and she moved backward, her hands behind her, trying to find something, anything she could use as a weapon.

"I don't know what you're talking about." She kept her gaze on him while she slowly moved in the direction of the bookcase. The cement flower pot was on one of the shelves. It was big and heavy.

He smiled while still coming closer. "You know. Or, if you don't know yet, you'll figure it out sooner or later. And I'd much rather you didn't. You see, the client your father phoned me about was someone I had approached with Hastings's product. By that time, I knew things were going south, and I knew I had to look after myself. So I duped this guy into believing he should make a payment directly to me, told him that was how things were done, and that I'd make the payments to the company."

Dana kept her gaze on Johnson while her hands found the heavy pot behind her back. Johnson kept talking. Was that sirens she was hearing?

"This guy talked to your dad about it, and of course your dad told him that no money should be paid to an advisor. I knew that if your dad told the financial services board about this on top of the whole Hastings thing, I'd never see the light of day again. So, I called in some favors, got your dad arrested, and had someone help him to leave this earth forever."

Dana caught her breath. He was confessing to organizing her dad's death! From far away, she could hear sirens.

Johnson put his hands around her throat. "So you see, Ms. Roux, I can't let you tell people what you are bound to find out. Surely, you understand that?" he asked, as if he was making perfect sense.

She couldn't hear any sirens now; she'd probably only imagined it. There was no help on the way as she'd hoped. It was up to her now whether she was going to live or die.

Dana got hold of the pot behind her with both hands. The front door burst open. Johnson turned, his hands dropped from around her neck, and she lifted the pot high above her head, ready to bring it down on his head as hard as she could.

DAVID WOULD NEVER forget the sight in front of him when he crashed through Dana's front door. The big man in front of his beloved had his hands around her throat. Her eyes were wild, her hair flying around her, and she stood like an avenging angel holding a big flower pot above her head. If she were afraid, he'd never have guessed it from the determined expression on her face.

The police were right behind him, guns at the ready, yelling loudly at the man who, now deathly pale, stumbled backward. He obviously hadn't been expecting anyone to come to Dana's rescue.

David reached Dana in two strides, and he gently took the flower pot from her hands where she was still holding it above her head. He pulled her shivering body close to his and fell in love with her all over again.

"It's over, sweetheart. Your window was open again, and we could hear everything he said. Grant Simpson, from what I could gather tonight, had his suspicions about Johnson being involved in your dad's death, but he didn't have any evidence. Now we have."

Dana pressed her face into his chest while the shivering slowly subsided. He held on tightly. Some of the policemen escorted Johnson from the house, while the detective hovered behind. But David didn't want to talk to anyone else just yet.

What had nearly happened to Dana tonight was only dawning on David now. He could have lost her. Never seen her again, never held her in his arms again.

"David, I'm okay," she whispered, wiggling in his arms.

He slackened his hold somewhat, realizing he'd had her in a death grip. "I'm sorry," he breathed into her hair. "He could have hurt you and I—"

He couldn't get another word past his throat. Instead, he caressed her back, trying to tell her with his hands how glad he was she wasn't hurt, how much he loved her.

From the corner of his eye, he saw the detective waving, trying to get his attention, but he wasn't quite ready to let go of Dana.

"What about Sam Jordan?" she asked.

The detective cleared his throat behind them. "That's what I'd like to talk to you about," he said.

"SO LET ME get this straight." Darryn frowned. "Johnson has been in jail for selling Hastings's Ponzi scheme, but nobody knew of his involvement in Dana's dad's death?"

The whole Cavallo clan had arrived early that morning at Don's house in Hermanus, and Caitlin's mother had hastened over.

It was a week later, but Dana still woke up at night, gasping for air. David had been a wonderful pillar over the past week and had waited until he had all the facts about Jordan and Johnson before he phoned his family.

Dale and Zoe had just arrived back from their honeymoon, and when they heard what had happened to Dana, they left their bags without unpacking and drove over.

Caitlin's mother's gaze took in Dana and David's entwined hands. The gleam in her eye only meant one thing— as soon as she could, she was going to take Dana aside and find out what she'd missed.

Dana looked around at her new family. She'd always felt much more at home at the Sutherlands than at her own home, especially after her dad's death. Now the Cavallos had also accepted her with hugs and kisses, and she already felt part of them.

The only person missing was Caitlin's other sister, Hannah. Nobody was sure where the model was at this specific point.

David explained and talked about what they knew, and Dana sat quietly next to him, still amazed at the way greed could change good people into bad ones.

The whole money laundering scheme had been revealed, which meant Hastings wasn't getting out of jail anytime soon, and Sam Jordan would join him in a matter of weeks.

"It's going to take some time to find the whole money trail, but Jordan's house was bought with cash. The particular details still have to be unraveled. But after Dana and I visited him and then she…" David glanced at her. He tried to sound cross. "Then she visited him again, he tried to flee the country. By that time, the police had been alerted, and he was taken into custody at the airport."

"So now what?" David's mother asked.

"Well, there is nothing more we can do; it's now over to the authorities. We'll have to wait for the whole judicial system to do its thing and, as we know, it doesn't work very quickly in this country. But I'm sure justice will be served. And I'm very glad that Dana here has the answers she's been looking for over the past two years."

Don shook his head. "The whole thing sounds like something out of a thriller, but I'm very glad you're okay, Dana. Things could have been so much worse."

"I know." She smiled up at David. "But your brother here came to my rescue." She looked around at all the worried faces. "Thank you all for being here. It means…" Her throat clogged up and she couldn't say another word.

Darryn, who was standing close by, patted her back. "You're family. Of course we're all here for you," he said gruffly.

And then everyone was talking together, asking more questions, giving her more hugs. And all the while, David had her hand in his, keeping her close to his side.

Chapter Nineteen

DANA COULD NEVER explain afterward exactly how all the women ended up in a coffee shop in Hermanus, but Caitlin's mom, Brenda, probably had a lot to do with it.

The setting was idyllic. The coffee shop was close to the old harbor, and from the terrace, the whole of Walker Bay lay in front of them. Back at Don's home, the men were making a fire for a barbecue later. There was still a niggling worry somewhere inside her, but for the moment she was ignoring it.

"I can't believe it's Christmas next week," Dana said. "So much has happened over the last few weeks."

"She wants to talk about Christmas." Caitlin smiled. "As if she doesn't have stars in her eyes in spite of everything that has happened."

Heat crept up her cheeks. "I—" she began, but didn't know what else to say, so she put her hands to her burning cheeks.

"So, tell me." Zoe giggled. "What has happened since my wedding? I left you scowling in David's direction, only to find you drooling over the guy a month later."

Dana laughed. "I don't know where to begin!"

"According to my mother-in-law here," Caitlin said with a twinkle in her eye, "David fell for her the moment he met her at Rosa's!"

Brenda beamed. "I knew it. There was just something in the way he looked at her, you remember?" she asked Rosa.

Rosa nodded, her eyes suspiciously bright. "I remember. It took him a while to figure it out, but I have complete faith that my boys will eventually choose the right partner. Well, except for Darryn," she said and frowned. "I worry about him."

"He'll come round," Brenda said before she turned to Dana again. "So Dana, when is the wedding?" she asked.

Dana blinked. "Um…"

Rosa threw a hand up. "Don't tell me—he hasn't said anything?"

Dana shook her head, not quite sure where the conversation was heading. But now she knew what that niggling thing was she'd been carrying around for the past few days.

She was happy with David, would be whatever he did, but… he hadn't said anything about marrying her. She was okay with that, but she had been thinking about it. A lot.

Didn't he want to get married? Or didn't he want to get married to her? And what happened if he met someone he did want to marry?

Zoe patted her hand. "Let's have cheesecake and stop worrying. These two," she said and pointed to the two mothers, "will sort it out."

THEY WERE ON their second beer when Don slapped him on the back. "So have you talked to Dale like I said you should or have you discovered all on your own what else you should do?"

Dale frowned. "What are you talking about?" Don laughed and waved Dale over to them.

"Come and tell our brother here what else he should do before we leave him to the mercy of Mom and Brenda."

Dale smiled. "You mean he also doesn't know what to do to make sure he gets the girl?"

By this time David felt like throwing his beer in their faces. "I got the girl—I don't know what you're talking about."

"Did you ask her to marry you?" Dale asked. "I mean in so many words?"

David opened his mouth to say he did but then realized he never used those specific words. "I told her I love her. Doesn't that include everything? I mean, of course, I want to marry her—why the hell would I tell her I loved her otherwise!"

Don and Dale laughed. Darryn grimaced.

Dale patted him on the shoulder. "You have a lot to learn. Lesson number one, you have to tell them what is going on in your mind. You have to spell things out, letter by letter, to make sure there is no misunderstanding."

"Surely she knows?" David asked, dazed.

"Welcome to the club of clueless husbands." Don smiled. "But you'll learn!"

"So what do I do?" he asked.

Don rolled his eyes. "Darryn, why don't you listen as well? Because one of these days, you'll also need to know the answer."

Darryn swore and walked in the direction of the kitchen. "I am the only sane one around. I'll fetch the meat for the barbecue," he said brusquely.

Don shrugged. "Well, then we'll tell you," he said and sat down next to David.

IT WAS LATE by the time David took her home.

He was very quiet, had been throughout the evening. Every time she had looked in his direction, his eyes had been on her, and he'd mostly stayed close, always finding ways to touch her.

David walked with her to her front door but didn't go in as he normally did. "Will you be okay on your own tonight?" he asked, and her heart sank.

"Why?" she began before she could stop herself. She swallowed. So this was his way of backing away. "Yeah, I'll be fine," she said, tears welling up in her eyes.

She quickly went into her house and started closing the

front door behind her, but David caught the door before it closed.

"I… there's something I have to do. Idiot that I am, I didn't know that I… that you… but I'll see you tomorrow. I love you." He kissed her. Possessively.

Before she could blink, he was gone. Slowly, she closed the door behind her. What was going on? He said he loved her, but he didn't want to stay with her? And what was it he had to do?

She was tired. All the emotions of the past few days that she had been keeping bottled up finally burst open, and the tears started to flow. She stumbled to her room and fell on the bed.

She'd always known her dad was innocent, but for so long she'd been the only one who believed that. Finding out that her beloved dad hadn't taken the easy way out, as so many people had accused him of, at least gave her some closure. That her kind and loving father had to die in such a brutal way would probably always haunt her, but at least now the people who were responsible for his untimely death were behind bars.

Hopefully, she'd pass out immediately. What exactly was going on she didn't know, and her brain was just too tired to try and figure it out at this stage.

David did kiss her, and he did tell her he loved her. That was all that really mattered though, wasn't it?

WHEN THE KNOCK on her front door came, she was showered, dressed, and had already had her first cup of coffee. She was ready for him.

She opened the door with a big smile. "Hi David. It's so nice to see you. Won't you come on in? I've made coffee," she babbled, and turning her back on his, she walked back to the kitchen.

His hand shot out and caught her arm, and the next moment he'd bent her over his arm and was kissing her thoroughly. Only when she could feel her legs turning to rubber did he lift his head, his eyes dark with desire. He pulled her up and put his hands on her hips.

"Apparently, there was one more thing I had to do. I thought you'd know, but my brothers tell me I still have to figure out how a woman's mind works. And I wasn't sure how to do it. I could make this grand gesture, wait for Christmas, put on a Santa suit on a hot day, take you to an island, have a plane fly over us with the question, write it on the sand at one of the beaches here in Hermanus, or I can just ask you."

She'd stop breathing at "apparently" and realized she had to get some oxygen into her lungs. Inhaling deeply, she put her hands on his shoulders.

"Ask me what?" she said.

"If you will marry me, damn it," he said crossly. "I assumed you'd know. I said I love you, of course I want to marry you!" he nearly shouted.

She swallowed a smile. Never again would she have this kind of upper hand.

Lifting her hand, she caressed his face. "No, I didn't know you also wanted to marry me. You have to ask me if that's what you want to do," she said solemnly.

Astonished, David looked at her. "But I just asked you!" he cried out, not quite sure what was going on. But then he saw the twinkle in her eyes, and his heart that had been pumping away at a ridiculous pace settled down.

"Ask me nicely," she commanded.

And he finally remembered all Don's and Dale's and his mother's coaching.

Patting his pocket, he got down on one knee.

Dana's eyes nearly popped out of her head.

"Dana Roux," he said and took out a little box from his pocket, "will you please marry me? Damn it, I didn't think it would be this difficult!"

She looked down at him, obviously stunned for a few minutes. "Why?" she asked, her eyes wide open.

And then the words were there—he knew exactly what to say.

"I've always followed my instincts with you. Kissing you was done on instinct, and I asked myself last night what would have happened if I'd never kissed you. I would never have known what it feels like when someone touches my essence, my core. But I listened, and now I know. And I don't want to live without that again. I love you, Dana. And it's a deep, irreversible, forever kind of love, so if you say yes, you're stuck with me for life."

And then she fell forward, into his arms, tears streaming over her face.

Alarmed, he touched her cheek. "What?"

She sniffed. "Happy tears, they're happy tears," she said brokenly and kissed him. "Of course I'll marry you. But why didn't you tell me last night? I was ready to send you away this morning. This whole process has taught me one thing—life is short and one stupid decision could change your whole life. I've decided I have a lot of love to give and I was going to tell you I want to get married, and if you didn't want to, I'd have to find someone who did."

"I didn't have the ring last night!" he cried. "Believe me, it was the hardest thing I had to do to leave you here alone. But I still had to get the bloody ring, and I could only do that this morning. Don knows the guy. He bought Caitlin's ring from him as well," he said, lifting the little box again. He fell backward dragging her with him so that she was lying on top of him.

She giggled and opened the box. For long minutes she stared at the ring but didn't say anything.

Worried, he pushed her hair out of her face. "If you don't like it, we can return it. There is just one jewelry store in Hermanus, and this is the only one I liked. I'll buy you a big, glittering diamond when we're back in Cape Town."

"I love it," she said, her eyes glistening with tears. "It's beautiful."

Slowly, he took the ring out of the box and put it on her ring finger. "Just please tell me I've done everything I should have now?" he nearly pleaded.

Slowly, she sat back on her haunches. "I'm afraid not," she said and lifted her top over her head. "You still have one more thing to do," she said, shoving his T-shirt upward.

She spread her hands over his chest and lowered her head. "Or maybe two, I'm not quite sure," she whispered against his skin.

Groaning, he lifted her up so he could claim her mouth. "Gladly. And I want to be very thorough, so this will take some time," he whispered against her mouth.

Epilogue

THE MUSIC SWELLED, and with her heart in her throat, Dana began to walk down the aisle on her brother's arm. She was so glad he was here today to give her away. Her mother was standing stiffly to one side, and on impulse, Dana stopped, took a pink rose out of her bouquet and gave it to her mother. This woman was her mother, and Dana loved her—she would probably never know why her mother did the things she did, but that was also okay.

Surprised, her mother took the rose and smelled it. When she looked up, her eyes were bright. Dana smiled at her before she and her brother continued walking down the aisle.

Two steps away, David, flanked by his brothers, was waiting for her. His eyes were on her, his smile devastating. She hurried forward, and her brother laughed.

"He can wait a little longer," he said under his breath.

"But I can't." She giggled.

DAVID'S SMILE BROADENED when he saw his bride walking a

little faster, and he moved forward as well. He also couldn't wait to give her his name.

Because she already had his heart, his soul, his very being.

He caught her hand, pulled her forward and framed her face with his hands. The pastor cleared his throat loudly. Everyone laughed, but he hadn't seen his bride all day, and he couldn't wait another second to kiss her.

Bending down, he caught her lips with his, and when her sweet, warm breath touched his face, he relaxed for the first time. He was following his instincts, like he did at Dale's wedding. He was going to kiss this woman now.

The End

If you enjoyed this book, please leave a review at your favorite online retailer!
Even if it's just a sentence or two it makes all the difference.

Thanks for reading *An Irresistible Temptation by Elsa Winckler*!

Discover your next romance at TulePublishing.com.

TULE
PUBLISHING

The Cavallo Brothers series

Book 1: *An Impossible Attraction*

Book 2: *An Irresistible Temptation*

Book 3: Coming soon

Available now at your favorite online retailer!

About the Author

I have been reading love stories for as long as I can remember and when I 'met' the classic authors like Jane Austen, Elizabeth Gaskell, Henry James The Brontë sisters, etc. during my Honours studies, I was hooked for life.

I married my college boyfriend and soul mate and after 43 years, 3 interesting and wonderful children and 3 beautiful grandchildren, he still makes me weak in the knees. We are fortunate to live in the picturesque little seaside village of Betty's Bay, South Africa with the ocean a block away and a beautiful mountain right behind us. And although life so far has not always been an easy ride, it has always been an exiting and interesting one!

I like the heroines in my stories to be beautiful, feisty, independent and headstrong. And the heroes must be strong but possess a generous amount of sensitivity. They are of course, also gorgeous! My stories typically incorporate the family background of the characters to better understand where they come from and who they are when we meet them in the story.

Thank you for reading

An Irresistible Temptation

If you enjoyed this book, you can find more from all our great authors at TulePublishing.com, or from your favorite online retailer.

TULE
PUBLISHING

Made in the USA
Coppell, TX
13 June 2023

18033150R00120